MONTANA
MATCH

MONTANA MATCH

•

Fran Shaff

AVALON BOOKS
NEW YORK

PRINTED IN THE UNITED STATES OF AMERICA
ON ACID-FREE PAPER
BY HADDON CRAFTSMEN, BLOOMSBURG, PENNSYLVANIA

For my cousin, David G.,
whose wise words made all the difference
and
For Dianna, whose friendship is warmer than cocoa

Chapter One

He's nothing like I expected, Becky thought as she pulled up in front of Jake Ruskin's Montana ranch house. She carefully eyed the man hanging laundry on the line in the backyard. Five feet, ten inches, she guessed, sixty, maybe sixty-three. She put the car in park, turned off the ignition and continued her distant inspection. Gray hair, nicely-groomed, full gray beard. He definitely didn't fit the picture of vitality she'd envisioned speaking to Jake on the phone. His deep, sexy voice had sent shivers through her—something that had never happened to her with any other client in fifteen years of matchmaking. She had been absolutely certain Jake Ruskin would be drop-dead gorgeous and as easy to mate with a prospective bride as anyone she'd ever matched before. Instead, the windfall Jake had promised her to find him a wife would not be easily earned.

Becky stepped from the car. She ran her hands over her turquoise linen business suit and adjusted the short skirt. The ankles poised over her matching pumps twisted as she stepped over the gravel driveway.

1

She stopped and glanced again at the gray-haired man hanging laundry. "Here goes nothing," she said, lifting her head and tossing her long black hair over her shoulders.

Becky took a few steps up the crumbling brick walkway toward the house, then tread on the lawn to access the backyard. The heels of her pumps instantly sunk into the wet sod. Becky pulled her feet free and stepped forward. She sunk into the earth again.

"Oh, no," she whispered. She looked around for an alternate route to the backyard. Short of going through the house, there wasn't one. She had to use the lawn. She lifted her leg, and her foot slipped out of the shoe. "Gosh almighty! There's no way I'm walking without my shoes and ruining my new hose." Becky stuffed her foot back into her shoe and tried again to loosen her pumps from the grasping ground.

She was about to let go of the expletive her failed progress pushed to the tip of her tongue when she suddenly felt herself being swept up. Powerful arms engulfed her and pressed her close to an equally muscular, rigid chest. Before she could say anything, he started scolding her.

"What do you think you're doing, Miss Montoya?" the man holding her shouted.

Becky stared into the icy blue eyes inches above her. Words stuck in her throat.

"You are Becky Montoya, aren't you?"

Becky still couldn't speak.

The strikingly handsome man with the thick, black hair that shimmered with flecks of gray shook his head in his obvious displeasure over Becky's silence and whisked her up the stairs, past the porch and over the threshold into the house. He set her down inside and folded his arms. "Well?"

"Y-yes," Becky stammered, pushing her jet-black hair over her shoulder. "I'm Becky Montoya." She pointed her thumb over her shoulder and glanced briefly behind her, then back at the man who'd just carried her into the house. "I'm here to see Mr. Ruskin. I saw him putting laundry up on the line in the backyard. He's expecting me."

The ice-blue eyes softened into an amused smile that spread over the robust, masculine face. The man rubbed his strong hands together before he stuffed them into his jeans pockets. A chuckle bubbled over his prominent Adam's apple. "You thought that Sam . . ." he said slowly.

Becky reached out and touched his arm. She wrinkled her forehead. "Oh, no, it isn't Sam Ruskin. I'm looking for Jake Ruskin." Isn't he," she said, pointing over her shoulder, "Jake Ruskin?"

"No, ma'am, I am," Jake said, extending his hand. "Disappointed?"

Becky reflexively took Jake's hand and hoped he couldn't feel the trembling coursing through her. She forced a smile. "I, I don't know what to say. I'm sorry about the mistake, Mr. Ruskin."

"You don't have to say anything, Miss Montoya. Sam'll get a kick out of it."

Becky jerked her hand from Jake's and lunged toward him, thrusting her hands against his rock-hard chest. "Oh, please, Mr. Ruskin, don't tell Mr. . . . ah, Sam about my mistake. I'm much too embarrassed about it already."

Jake placed his hands over hers. He nodded slowly.

"Okay, Miss Montoya. I won't tell Sam." His eyes narrowed.

Becky glanced from his deliberate gaze toward her hands on his chest and his hands on top of hers. She freed herself of him and stepped back. Suddenly she became aware of the feel of a rug under her stockinged feet. She cast her eyes downward. "My shoes." She shifted her gaze toward the window.

"Yes, about those shoes," Jake said, folding his arms, "and those clothes." He slowly moved his inspecting eyes over her. "I hope you brought plenty of jeans and a good strong pair of boots. Feminine stockings, and skirts and high heels won't do on a ranch." He lifted a finger to his chin and spread an amused grin over his tanned face. "I guess perhaps you've learned that already."

Becky straightened her stance and stood to her full five feet, seven inches. "You needn't worry. I have both jeans and sneakers packed for my visit here."

"Sneakers?" Jake shook his head. "You aren't here to play tennis, Miss Montoya. If you intend to follow me around as part of your research about me, you're going to need a good pair of boots." He stepped toward her and took her arm. "Come with me."

"Where are we going?" she asked as he dragged her to the open staircase.

"Up to my office to get you a pair."

"Your office? You keep extra boots in your office?" His hand rested on the small of her back as he guided her up the stairs.

"I can get anything I want from my office. I bet you can from yours too."

As they neared the top of the stairs, Becky said, "Well, yes, but my office is in the loop in Chicago."

She stopped and turned toward him. "Yours is in the middle of nowhere."

Jake took her arm and led her down the hall. "My dear Miss Montoya, in the twenty-first century no place with a phone line and electricity is in the middle of nowhere." He opened the door to his office, released her and went straight to his computer. In a matter of seconds he was on line. He turned to her. "Now what size boots would you like?"

"Seven and a half."

Jake glanced at her feet. "I would have said eight. Are you sure seven and a half will be comfortable? You'll be doing a great deal of walking."

Becky defiantly folded her arms. "I certainly don't need you to tell me my own shoe size."

Jake turned back to the computer screen and made a few clicks.

"You'll need my credit card," Becky said, opening the small handbag she had slung over her shoulder.

Jake waved his hand. "Consider it part of the uniform your employer is providing." He clicked again. "Is there anything else you need?" he asked, looking at her.

Becky shook her head.

He focused again on the monitor and finished his transaction. "All right. The boots will be here tomorrow morning—not as quick as running into a store on State Street or Michigan Avenue, but sufficiently fast."

Becky folded her arms and smiled. "You're pretty efficient on that computer. Do you use it a lot?"

Jake stretched to his full height which Becky estimated in the six-feet, four-inch range. "Now that is quite an amusing question coming from you, Miss

Montoya. Didn't I hire you to use your computer to find me a wife?"

Color burned in Becky's cheeks. "You don't flatter my job when you refer to it in such impersonal terms, Mr. Ruskin. I do much more than merely use a machine to couple a man and woman together in a life-long relationship."

Jake slid his hand to her back and returned her to the top of the stairs. As they began to descend, he said, "For what I'm paying you, I expect much more from you than I could ever get from a computer."

Becky stopped and looked up at the man behind her. Her lips curved upwards. "You needn't worry about getting what you want from me, Mr. Ruskin. Before I leave, I'll know you well enough to find the perfect woman for you."

Jake nodded as he covered his face with a doubtful grin. "The perfect woman, huh? My *'Match Made in Heaven'*?" he asked, quoting the name of her business.

Becky chuckled and tucked her hair behind her ears. "There's a rather amusing story behind that name. The suite where my first office opened fifteen years ago was number HVN—H for suite H, V for being on the fifth floor and N because it was on the north side of the building. My assistant suggested the name *Match Made in Heaven* because of the HVN suite number, but, no matter what the name of my business, I guarantee you'll be satisfied with your selection. It's all very scientific, and you know how successful I am or you never would have hired me. Isn't that right, Mr. Ruskin?"

He slipped his arm around her shoulders as they reached the bottom of the stairs and led her to the sofa.

"We'll see, Miss Montoya. For now, why don't you make yourself comfortable while I see what Sam has for us to drink in the kitchen?"

As Jake left the room, Becky sunk into the mahogany-colored leather sofa. She took advantage of Jake's absence to familiarize herself with his parlor. Homey, she decided, but modern. The huge stone fireplace warmed by a dark walnut mantle contrasted with the big-screen television a few feet away from it. On the old-fashioned hooked rug ahead of the hearth were two wooden rockers, each with a patchwork quilt over its back. The leather couch and recliner were flanked by walnut end tables, and they encircled a large matching walnut coffee table. Grand windows lay symmetrically on either side of the front door. A small walnut table rested under each window. On top of the tables were matching antique china vases. Becky glanced back to the fireplace. Above the mantle hung an oil painting. She stood and walked to it to inspect it further. It was a pastoral by an artist she didn't recognize. She found the work primitive but intriguing. It had included odd little animals she'd never seen in countryside painting before.

As she seated herself on the sofa, Jake came into the room with two glasses of soda. He handed one to her. "Well, what have you surmised about me so far?" he asked, waving his free hand around the room.

Becky sipped from her glass and set it on a coaster. "Well," she said, nodding and glancing around, "I've learned a few things." She rubbed her hand on the leather. "You obviously like furniture that is as finely crafted as it is comfortable."

Jake seated himself in the recliner and listened.

"You're not averse to owning fine china antiques."

She pointed toward the vases near the windows. She glanced at the floor. "You appreciate hardwood enough to have not carpeted over it. You like modern conveniences," she noted, pointing to the big-screen television, "but not so much that you'd convert your old-fashioned stone fireplace to a low-maintenance gas burner." She gave him a quizzical look and tilted her head. "Is it the romance of a crackling fire that keeps you from installing a more efficient way of warming the room or have you just never gotten around to making the change?"

"Romance?" Jake laughed heartily. "I build a fire to keep warm. I don't care how much more *efficient* a gas fireplace may or may not be. When I fill my hearth with *real* logs I want a fire that'll burn hot enough to keep me warm in my BVD's in the middle of January."

Becky had to look away. The picture she conjured of Jake in his underwear scorched her as though there were a fire burning in the room as hot as Jake described. He was no dowdy cowboy. That was for sure. She stood and walked to the hearth. She touched the painting and turned to Jake. "This piece puzzles me." She looked back at the picture. "It's not a collector's item like the vase, nor an indulgence in luxury like the furniture or the television." She felt Jake settle directly behind her. She turned and looked up at him as he hovered over her. "It isn't even a particularly beautiful work. Why did you place it here?"

Jake raised his arm over her and touched the frame. "I have my reasons," he said, staring at the country scene.

Becky saw a curious intensity grow in Jake's eyes, yet she couldn't help but press him further. "Who is

Rusty, and why did he sign only one name to his work?"

Jake moved his hand from the frame to the mantle. He placed his remaining palm on the other side of Becky, enclosing her between him and the hearth. His intense gaze moved from the painting to her. "I know you're here to learn about me, Miss Montoya," he said, his voice even huskier than normal, "but you don't need to know everything. Do you understand that?"

Becky could barely swallow under his power. "Of course, Mr. Ruskin," she managed to say through shallow breaths.

He touched a finger under her chin. "Good." He backed away from her.

Becky turned and gasped for breath as inconspicuously as she could when Jake stepped away. She cleared her throat. "You just let me know if I'm stepping into territory where I don't belong. My intention isn't to pry no matter how much it might sometimes look like that's what I'm doing."

Jake chuckled and stuffed his thumbs into his back pockets. "All right, Miss Montoya, I'll tell you when you're in uncharted area."

Becky smiled. "Good . . . and speaking of charts, I should get mine and start making it yours."

Jake tilted his head. "You're all business, aren't you? I like that," he said, nodding. "Normally, that is, but not at the moment." He took Becky's arm. "Before we go any further, I'd like you to meet Sam. He takes care of the house and cooks meals so you'll be seeing a lot of him."

"Yes, of course," Becky said.

"Incidentally, as far as anyone here knows, you're

an old friend visiting from Chicago. I don't tell the people who work for me my personal business."

"You can trust me, Mr. Ruskin. I'm completely reliable."

Jake stopped in the kitchen and narrowed his gaze toward her. "I'm counting on that." He turned to the back door and opened it. "Sam!" he yelled. "Come in here."

In a matter of seconds Sam filled the frame of the back door. "You called, boss?"

"Sam," Jake said, circling next to Becky and placing his hand on her spine, "this is Miss Becky Montoya. She's a friend of mine visiting from Chicago. She's going to be here a week or so."

Sam thrust his hand toward Becky. "Sam Bunker—like the hill."

Becky shook his hand. "Glad to know you, Mr. Bunker."

"Oh, no, not Mr. Bunker, ma'am," Sam said sheepishly. "It's Sam. Anything you need, ma'am, you just tell old Sam. I'll have it for you in a jiffy." Turning to Jake he said, "Would you like me to check on the guest room now, Mr. Jake?"

"The guest room, oh, no," Becky interrupted. "I'll be staying at a hotel."

Their laugh came in unison, Jake's deep and throaty, Sam's high-pitched and raspy.

"She thinks she's still in the city, Mr. Jake."

The cowboy turned to Becky. "I'm afraid the nearest hotel is fifty miles from here, Miss Montoya. I probably should have made that clear. I guess I shouldn't have assumed you understood that you were invited to stay here in the house."

Becky felt as flushed as a teenager getting caught

by her father as she received her first kiss. "Oh, goodness, I should have realized." She looked at Sam. "You're right, Sam, I'm thinking like a city woman. I'll have to change that while I'm here, won't I?"

Sam grinned broadly. "Something tells me you'll do that real easy, ma'am. I got a feeling you're going to fit right in."

"Thank you, Sam. I don't know about fitting in, but I'll try. I can assure you of that."

Jake pressed his hand into Becky's back and turned her round. Calling over his shoulder, he said, "We'll see you for supper, Sam." Then to Becky, "Six all right with you, Miss Montoya?"

Becky tried to stifle the yawn that insisted on preceding her reply, but she couldn't do it. "Six, yes, that's fine."

"First things first," Jake said, taking Becky through the living room and opening the front door. "I'll get your things and show you to your room. You look like you could use a nap."

Becky lunged toward Jake as he stepped out the front door. "Let me help you."

Jake put up his hands and caught her wrists. He stepped her back away from the door. "I don't think so, Miss Montoya." He glanced downwards, then grinned into Becky's surprised gaze. "You wouldn't want to ruin those city stockings on country cobblestones."

Becky eyed the brick sidewalk, then smiled at Jake. "I guess not." She reached into her purse. "Here are the keys for the trunk. I'll need the large case, the small one and the bag with the notebook computer."

Jake turned to descend the stairs. "And the two shoes stuck in the lawn," he called over his shoulder.

In a few minutes the cowboy and the matchmaker were in the third bedroom of Jake's two-story, eighty-plus-year-old ranch home. Becky surveyed her new surroundings. "Very nice, Mr. Ruskin. It's different from the rest of the house." She looked up at Jake who stood a breath behind her. "Why?"

His dark gaze instantly told her she was once again out of line. He lifted a shoulder. "Just is."

She didn't press him. She returned her eyes to the furnishings of the room. Light shades of lavender and pink touched the white background of the bedspread and Priscilla curtains. The walls were filled with all kinds of small items—photos, cross-stitching, painted wood, punched metal and copper pictures, etchings, dried flowers circled by wood hoops. The decor gave a feeling of brightness and artistic, natural charm. Becky felt instantly at home. "It's quite lovely. I'm going to enjoy it here." She stepped closer to the wall and started an inspection past the intriguing knick-knacks.

"Looking for something in particular?"

"A phone line. I'll need a phone and, of course, I'll need the line for the computer as well."

"It's on the other side of the desk. I think you'll find you have everything you need." He pointed when she turned round to look at him. "The bathroom's through that door. It's shared with the bedroom I use for my office so you'll have complete privacy. Sam's bedroom and bathroom are downstairs and mine are farther down the hall."

"Well," Becky said, folding her arms and walking toward her host, "I hadn't expected such lavish accommodations. Thank you, Mr. Ruskin."

"Like the boots, it all comes with the job."

She was standing only inches from him, looking up at him, studying what kind of man he might be. She'd categorized hundreds of men over the last fifteen years of her practice, probably thousands.

Jake tilted his head and lifted his hand. He touched his fingers to the hair lying close to Becky's graceful neck and lifted the silken strands off her shoulder.

A shudder coursed through Becky from her fingertips to her toes. Jake possessed her eyes. Her heartbeat was approaching mach speed.

He slid his fingers through her long, black tresses once more, holding her with his eyes.

"Mr. Ruskin," Becky heard herself say.

The sound of her voice stirred him. He quickly dropped his gaze and stepped back. "Fuzz," he said, wiping a finger over his lip. "You had a piece of fuzz in your hair from the afghan lying over the rocker. You must have brushed against it when you were looking for the phone jack."

Becky nodded and self-consciously tugged at her hair. "Oh, thanks."

Jake backed toward the door. "I'll see you at six, for supper. Shall I come get you?"

"No, I'll be fine." Becky shook her head and smiled. Another yawn escaped her.

"Rest a while. We can get down to business right after supper, if you feel up to it, okay?"

Becky nodded. "See you at six."

Jake turned and closed the door.

Releasing a deep breath, she sat on the bed and lay back against a stack of pillows. Jake Ruskin, client, seeking a wife. Becky touched her hair again where Jake had caressed it. Another shudder shook her body. He's a client. I'm not allowed to be attracted to him,

Becky admonished herself. Getting involved with Jake in an unprofessional way would be a bigger mistake than draining Lake Michigan, and just as impossible.

Jake went from Becky's room to the kitchen for a cup of coffee. He poured and sat at the table of the empty room, grateful for a moment alone without his talkative housekeeper freely giving his opinions. He took a long sip of the strong black brew. Becky Montoya was one beautiful woman. He hadn't expected a matchmaker to be so attractive. He'd envisioned a fifty-something busybody that would drive him to distraction.

Jake took another sip of steaming coffee. Miss Montoya would definitely drive him to distraction, but not for the reason he'd imagined.

He stretched his strong arms over his head, brought his elbows back to the table, and grinned. The moment he saw her struggling to get her heels out of his wet lawn, he wanted her in his arms. The mere sight of her had been like a kick in the gut. In the name of rescue, he seized his opportunity and swept her up close and whisked her into his house. Over their next moments together he'd used every occasion he could to get close to her, touching her in any way possible without insulting her—up the stairs, in his office, down the stairs, near the fireplace, up in her bedroom.

Jake raked his fingers through his thick, dark, gray-flecked hair. In her bedroom—he nearly pulled her into his arms right there and kissed her. He wondered if she tasted half as good as she smelled.

Quickly, Jake poured the remaining hot coffee into himself and bolted from the table. He went to the sink and rinsed the cup before placing it in the dishwasher.

He leaned over the sink and looked out the window, stretching to see Becky's car. She could be married, for all he knew, or engaged or whatever.

The back door slammed. "Mr. Jake, you want something?"

Jake snapped his head toward Sam's voice. "No, Sam, I'm fine. Just had a cup of coffee."

"Can I get you anything else?"

"No." Jake looked again at Becky's car.

In a moment Sam stood next to him. "She's a right fine woman, Mr. Jake."

The cowboy looked down at Sam who was staring out the window. "Miss Montoya?"

Sam shifted his eyes to his boss. "Real pretty, ain't she? How long you known her?"

"Not long."

"How'd you two meet? I mean her bein' from Chicago and all."

Jake stretched to his full height. "You're getting a little curious again, Sam. Don't you have something else to do?"

"You always see to it I'm busy from sunup to sundown, boss, but that don't mean I don't have eyes to see when something funny is goin' on around here."

Jake folded his arms. "There's nothing funny going on around here. A nice young woman has come for a little visit. She's never been on a ranch, and I offered to show her around. Period."

Sam pointed toward the back door. "And that new Hereford bull out there is gonna have twin pigs."

Jake smiled and strode to the hat rack next to the door. He covered his head with his Stetson and grinned back at Sam. "Whatever you say, Sam."

Sam hurried to the door as Jake started to close it.

He held it open and called to his boss, "I say there's something fishy goin' on around here, like you and she got something goin' on between you."

Jake walked down the steps and over the path toward the barn.

Sam upped the decibel level of his voice as his boss put distance between them. "And I say it's about time."

Jake heard his nosy housekeeper laugh just before he slammed the door. The cowboy shook his head and began to wonder if now he might just have two matchmakers in his house.

Chapter Two

When Becky woke from her nap, it was nearly six. She bolted from bed into the bathroom. She washed her face to wake herself up. She didn't bother replacing her makeup. Jake had told her to be casual, and she was extending that to include a lack of makeup. She slid out of her wrinkled suit and into a pair of jeans and a bright yellow T-shirt. She combed through her straight hair and flung it over her shoulders. Glancing in the mirror she noticed an eyelash resting on one of her cheeks. She wiped her hand over her light bronze skin and smiled at her casual reflection. Perhaps now she would look more country and less city.

Becky found Sam in the kitchen putting the finishing touches on his meal. "Hello, Sam. It smells wonderful in here."

Sam jerked his head around as he pulled the last baked potato from the oven. "Evenin', Miss Montoya." He straightened and kicked the oven door shut. "Mm, don't you look pretty."

Becky bowed slightly. "Why, thank you, Sam. I fig-

17

ured the jeans would make me look a little more country."

"I don't know about lookin' country in those Levis,
but I do know I never seen a pair of jeans look better."

Becky laughed softly. "Why thank you, Sam. Can
I help you with the dinner?"

"Everything's done."

Becky glanced at the empty table. "Perhaps I could
set the table."

"Already done." Sam put the potatoes in a bowl.
"I've just got to go out to the grill and fetch the steaks.
Be back in a jiffy." He'd barely left the kitchen when
he returned with a platter of thick steaks.

"That looks sinfully delicious," Becky said, admir-
ing Sam's handiwork.

"Ain't nothing sinful about it—just good American
beef. We grow it right here. Best in the world." Sam
ushered Becky to a chair at the small kitchen table.
"Now," he said, seating himself opposite her, "speaking of the best in the world, I got to tell you something
about Mr. Jake. They don't come any better than him,
ma'am. You got yourself a real number-one man there,
and you shouldn't let him get away." He reached over
to touch Becky's fingers. "Ma'am, Miss Montoya, I
seen him lookin' at you when you wasn't lookin'.
You're a lot more than just some friend from Chicago.
Mr. Jake likes you real fine."

"Sam, wait," Becky said, holding up her hand. "I'm
afraid you have the wrong idea. Mr. Ruskin and I are
more business associates than anything else. There is
absolutely nothing personal in our relationship."

Sam shook his head. "Missy, I wasn't born yesterday. I seen lots of hein' and shein' in my life. You
ain't no more mere business associates than I was with

my late wife. Mr. Jake's got an eye for you, and I say it's about time."

Becky stood and stepped toward Sam. She put her hand on his shoulder. "I'm sure you're a very intuitive man, Sam, but this time you're wrong. I assure you Mr. Ruskin and I are not and will not be personally involved. Nothing in the world could be more impossible. Think about it," she said, folding her arms and leaning against the counter. "He's Montana and ranches and cattle and horses. I'm Chicago and high-rises and four-star restaurants. He's jeans and work shirts and boots. I'm business suits and high heels and formal gowns in the evening." She studied the older man's face in anticipation of his reaction. "Do you see what I mean? We don't fit in each other's worlds. A city person like me could no more become a country person than Mr. Ruskin could if he'd have been a city person. People don't change that much. I hope that shows you how silly your illusion about us is."

Sam nodded and turned to put the remaining food into bowls. "Missy?" He circled his gaze back to her. "Did you know Mr. Jake used to work on Wall Street in New York City? Did it for nearly ten years." He ran his eyes over her one more time, then settled his gaze on hers. "And you're wearing jeans now too."

Becky snapped from the counter and straightened her spine. "I think I'll go find your boss." Her exit couldn't have been quick enough to suit her. Within seconds she was in the living room opening the front door. She caught Jake bounding up the walkway.

"My, my," he said, his glance surveying her curves in the casual wear. When his gaze rested on her dark eyes he said, "You look like you had a nice rest."

Becky lifted a shoulder nonchalantly. "I feel better, thank you."

"Does Sam have supper ready?" Jake asked, stepping into the house with Becky.

"He does, and it looks delicious—steak, potatoes, fruit salad, green beans, dinner rolls—do you eat like this all the time or are these company vittles?"

"Vittles?" Jake asked, lifting a brow as a grin covered his face. "She not only looks a little less city, she talks a little more country too." He headed for the stairs. "I'll go wash up and be right back. Seat yourself on the sofa. I won't be long."

A few minutes later, Sam entered the living room. "I thought I heard Mr. Jake in here."

Becky rose from her seat on the couch. "You did. He went upstairs to wash up for dinner, I mean supper."

"I'm right here, Sam," Jake said as he descended the open staircase. He sported a fresh shirt and jeans and a gray tweed blazer. Becky smiled at his casual attempt to dress for dinner.

"Fine. I've got everything set up for you and Miss Montoya. I'm servin' in the dining room tonight. You know the way, Mr. Jake. You take her right in." In a flash, Sam had disappeared back into the kitchen.

Jake came to Becky and offered her his arm. "Miss Montoya?"

Becky laced her fingers around his biceps and went with him into the dining room. As they entered the darkened room lit only by candlelight, a chuckle bubbled from deep inside Jake.

Becky knew in an instant why Jake was laughing. Sam had created a thoroughly romantic ambiance for their dinner. Becky turned her gaze up to meet Jake's.

"I think you could have saved yourself a lot of money, Mr. Ruskin."

Jake wrinkled his brows. "Excuse me?"

Becky curved one side of her mouth upwards and flickered sparkling eyes at him. "It looks to me like you already had a matchmaker in the house."

"Sam?" Jake pointed a thumb toward the kitchen.

Becky nodded slowly. "Sam. He seems to have some idea that you and I are more than just friends or business associates. I tried to straighten him out before you came back, but apparently," she said, turning toward the table and waving her hand over it, "he didn't believe me."

Jake took Becky's hand from his biceps. He moved toward the window and raised the shade. "I'm sorry, Miss Montoya."

Becky pulled the blind on the other window and lightened the room further. "Don't worry about it, Mr. Ruskin. No harm's done, and I think Sam's enjoying himself with his little fantasy. I bet he does this kind of thing to you all the time." Becky stepped next to Jake and folded her arms. "Are you sure you need me?"

Jake touched her cheek and gazed at her with intense, icy eyes. "I'm sure." He reached for a chair and held it as Becky seated herself. Then he sat around the corner of the table near her. He tilted his head and creased his brows. "Miss Montoya, do you mind if I ask you a few questions before you start your inquisition of me?"

Becky shrugged. "I guess not, as long as I can reserve the right not to answer anything I don't want to."

"That's fair," Jake said, folding his hands and rais-

22   *Fran Shaff*

ing them to his lips as he leaned back in his armed chair. "First of all, I'm curious. Has the matchmaker made a match for herself?"

Becky sipped some iced tea. "My goodness, Mr. Ruskin, you don't believe in working up to something, do you?"

"And you, Miss Montoya, are avoiding the question."

"Touché," she said, smiling as she indulged in another taste of tea. Meeting Jake's intense eyes she replied, "No, the matchmaker has never made herself a match."

Jake moved his folded hands away from his mouth to speak. "Why? Is it a little like a doctor not healing himself or a lawyer not representing himself?"

Becky threw a mop of hair over her shoulder and leaned back in her chair. She shook her head. "Not at all. The matchmaker simply isn't interested in pairing up with anyone for any kind of permanent commitment."

He sprang forward and placed his arms on the table. "You can't be serious! A magnificent-looking woman like you? Why on earth not?"

Becky leaned ahead, elbow on the table, chin in her palm. She tilted her head up to meet Jake's gaze. "Mr. Ruskin, I think it would be very rude of us to let Sam's lovely dinner get cold before we enjoy it, don't you?"

"I'm treading where I don't belong." Jake lifted the platter of steaks and deposited one on Becky's plate and one on his own. "Perhaps I should change the subject."

"I think that would be a good idea." Becky reached for the bowl of potatoes and took one. "After dinner, I mean supper, I'll ask the questions, and we'll get started with taking care of the business you hired me to handle."

The meal they shared was no ordinary business meeting. Becky couldn't help but notice Jake's penetrating gaze fixed on her throughout each course. He wasn't the first client who'd been attracted to her. After all, men who used her services were looking for a woman, and she had been told most of her life that she wasn't hard on a man's eyes. The problem she hadn't experienced before was that she rather enjoyed Jake's attraction to her. In fact, if he weren't a client, if she'd met him outside of business, she'd be flirting with him right now, enticing him, encouraging him. Certainly any serious relationship with him would be out of the question since she'd sworn herself to the single life, but she would most definitely allow herself to enjoy his company for as long as possible. Jake Ruskin was incredibly attractive, and he'd make someone a great husband.

When their plates were empty, Jake led Becky to the living room. He gestured for her to make herself comfortable on the sofa, and he sat next to her. Becky turned on the lamp next to the couch and reached for the folder she'd left on the coffee table.

As she opened the folder and took out a pen, she turned to Jake. "Are you sure you want to work here? Sam could overhear us, and you did say you want to keep the purpose of my visit confidential."

Jake glanced toward the kitchen. Sam had already started cleaning up their supper dishes. He looked back at Becky. "Maybe you're right. Let's go up to my office."

Becky nodded and closed her folder. Jake helped

her from the sofa and guided her up the stairs, gently pressing his hand into her lower back.

A loveseat sat opposite the big oak desk in Jake's office. It barely accommodated the two of them. "Will this be okay?" Jake asked, lifting his massive arm to the back of the tiny sofa to give the two of them a little more room.

Becky settled into a comfortable position. "Fine, Mr. Ruskin."

Jake reached across Becky to turn on the lamp next to the loveseat, encircling her with his body. "How's that?"

Her breath caught under his power, and she wished they had stayed in the living room where the quarters weren't quite so confining. "It's, ah, fine," she said, clearing her throat and turning her attention to her folder.

Jake pulled his arm back from the lamp and nestled himself in the deep cushions.

Becky took her pen and tucked her hair behind her ears. "Are you ready to get started?"

"Shoot."

"All right, first of all, I'd like you to describe what attracts you physically in a woman." She stared at the form ahead of her and gripped her pen.

"Well . . . ," Jake paused.

Becky could feel his eyes on her.

"I'd say I'd find a woman with long black hair, dark eyes, light bronze skin and coming up to my chin quite attractive."

Becky slowly turned toward her cowboy client, a mock grin covering her face. She raised an eyebrow.

"But I'd also like a blond with blue eyes and about five and a half feet tall or a redhead six feet tall with sharp green eyes." Jake shifted uncomfortably. "Miss Montoya, I feel like a darn fool talking about this stuff. Especially to a woman."

Becky placed a comforting hand on his knee. "Please, relax, Mr. Ruskin. I know this isn't easy." She tilted her head thoughtfully. "Let's approach this from a different angle. Maybe you could tell me why you are looking for a wife. You know, why now, and why this way. Perhaps that would put you a little more at ease if you took me into your confidence. I've found that it sometimes helps clients to talk about what they are looking for and why."

Jake bolted from the loveseat and moved to his desk chair. He rolled it closer to the sofa and rested his elbows on the arms of the chair. "That might make it easier."

"Okay," Becky said, closing her folder and placing it along with her pen on the end table next to her. "Let's just talk."

Jake shifted in his chair. "As you probably guessed from the large fee I offered you, I am a rather wealthy man. I earned a fortune shortly after college when I worked on Wall Street. I had a knack for business. When my father died shortly after I turned thirty-one, I came back to the ranch where I grew up to sell it. Dad had let it go, and it wasn't even solvent anymore. When I got here, though, I changed my mind about selling. I decided to stay on and turn things around, but I wasn't about to give up my Wall Street way of life completely. Fortunately, with instant communication available," he said, nodding toward his computer, "I could continue to live in both worlds—both stock markets."

Becky grinned at his pun. "Each of them hopefully containing a strong bull."

"Exactly. I have continued to do very well, but I've devoted most of my time to business and very little to a social life." Jake sat forward and raised a hand toward Becky. "Don't get me wrong, Miss Montoya, I haven't been living like a monk. Although women are scarce in this part of Montana, I have managed to date from time to time. I've even had a serious relationship or two, but the timing was bad. I wasn't ready to settle into anything permanent."

"And now that you are, you're not in a relationship."

"It's a little more complicated than that." Jake stood and walked over to the window next to the sofa. He placed his hand high on the molding and stared out on his ranch. "I haven't any family—no children, no one to inherit what I've spent my life building." He turned and leaned against the oak that surrounded the window. He folded his arms and pierced his eyes toward Becky. "I need an heir. In order to have an heir, I need a wife."

Becky hoped she covered her shock sufficiently as she replied to his completely unexpected explanation. "I see." She'd assumed that Jake, like most of her clients, was a lonely man searching for love and companionship.

"I'd like someone I can get along with, naturally, but I have very specific ideas as to the arrangement I want to make with the woman who will agree to marry me and give me at least one child, more if she will."

"It sounds like you're looking for a business arrangement more than a marriage. You're not interested in love or companionship or intimacy beyond what it takes to merely produce children?" Becky kept her tone business-like and even.

"I guess you could say that, but I don't want to sound completely heartless. It isn't that I wouldn't enjoy or be interested in a traditional marital relationship, it's more that I don't expect to find it." A nervous chuckle bubbled over his Adam's apple, and Jake returned to his desk chair. "I suppose that sounds totally off the wall to a person like you. A matchmaker must be all romance and happy endings. After all, that's what you're pitching with your business, isn't it?"

Becky leaned her elbow on the arm of the little sofa. She placed her cheek in her palm. "I'll let you in on a little secret, Mr. Ruskin. I don't believe in 'happily ever after' any more than you do. While some people claim they find mates that set them on fire with passion, I don't believe such deep feelings exist beyond momentary infatuation. My own parents taught me just how miserable marriage can be and how much worse divorce can make it. That's the reason I won't ever marry myself, but it's also the reason I started my business. I do believe for the majority of people, marriage is the only way. For anyone willing to risk a completely committed relationship, I want to see them compatible enough to stay together and enjoy their union as long as they live."

"You make your calling sound very noble," Jake said, folding his arms.

"Noble?" Becky adjusted her position on the sofa. "To me it seems purely logical. If a person is going to marry, he or she should commit to someone they can at least tolerate. That doesn't sound noble to me. It sounds like good business."

"And business has been good for both you and your clients?"

"You've seen my success record, Mr. Ruskin. As for my clients, the divorce rate among them over the last fifteen years is well below the national average. For the entire period it is only fifteen percent—at least thirty-five percent lower than the national average. While I believe that's quite significant, I intend to see that rate plummet even further."

"Fifteen percent," Jake said, nodding and stroking his chin with his fingers. "Very impressive. However, I have no intention of letting divorce be an option with my wife, at least not until my children are raised. It will all be spelled out in the arrangement."

Becky opened her folder and took her pen. "All right, Mr. Ruskin, tell me about this arrangement you've been speaking of."

"As I said, I'd like you to find a woman who will be companionable for me. As you get to know me and my way of life over the next few days, you ought to be able to understand what type of woman would suit me. That's your area of expertise. What my prospective wife should know is what I expect of her."

Jake rose and returned to the sofa, resting his arm on the back as he had before. "I require a woman who will give me children and who will stay around long enough to raise them to adulthood. If she prefers, I'll provide her with separate living quarters, perhaps a small house of her own on my property. She may have whatever help she wishes, maid, nanny, even a chauffeur and a limo, if she wants. She can live in whatever luxury she may require as long as she's a good mother to my children. As for a career, I have no objection to her involving herself in business either as long as it doesn't demand too much of her time away from the children. She's free to have a life as separate from mine as she would like with one exception—our relationship must be strictly monogamous. I won't have her damage the family's reputation. I want no black marks against any of my children."

Becky finished writing, then glanced up at the man sitting so close beside her. "You've made yourself very clear, Mr. Ruskin. You've obviously thought about this for some time."

"I'm forty-three years old, Miss Montoya. I don't want to be an old man by the time my children are old enough to learn about the ranching business. I haven't time to wait around looking for Miss Right on my own. Believe me, I would much prefer having the luxury of falling in love the old-fashioned way and sharing my life with a woman I couldn't bear to be away from for even an hour, but I'm a hard-headed businessman, not a romantic schoolboy. So I approach my problem of producing an heir from that businessman's angle—hire an expert and use her to find the solution."

Becky replaced the pen in the folder and closed it firmly. "I think I understand what you want, Mr. Ruskin, and I'm sure I'll be able to help you."

Jake snapped to his feet. "Fine. Then our business is over for the day." He took Becky's hand and helped her to her feet. "Would you like to turn in for the evening?"

"Not yet," Becky said, stifling a yawn. "It is getting late, especially with the time difference for me on my first day here, but there's something I'd like to do before I call it a day."

"Something I can help with?"

"I don't need any help with it, but I'd love the company, if you'd like to come along."

Jake slipped his arm around her shoulders and aimed her towards the door. "It would be my pleasure. Just tell me where we're going."

Becky looked up at the azure eyes above her. "I want to see Montana's Big Sky at night."

Chapter Three

The evening air was cool for mid-June, and the sky sparkled with tiny glistening lights. The half-full moon shimmered silver splendor over the lightly rustling leaves of the ancient trees near the house.

Becky slipped away from Jake's protective arm and walked out into the yard. She looked high overhead and turned in a circle. "I don't believe it," she whispered barely loud enough for Jake to hear.

Jake watched in fascination. He knew what she meant, but he asked anyway. "What don't you believe?"

Becky stared upwards a moment longer, then fixed her eyes on Jake's. "The sky. I've seen it a million times. But I've never seen it like this." She looked up again. "The stars are like jewels. They're so intense, so vibrant. I want to look and look and memorize every perfect detail."

Jake could hardly believe the woman carrying on in such childish delight was the same pure-business executive he'd met with seconds ago. What a pleasure the next week would be having her around. Beauty, intelligence, warmth as deep as the sea and amusing naiveté about country life—all of it lay within Becky's business facade. She was here to learn about him, but he'd be learning about her too.

"Would you like to take a walk?" Jake asked, stepping next to his guest.

"I'm afraid I'd fall over something. All I want to do is look up," she replied, laughing. She turned and looked at Jake. "I'm acting like a silly child at a fireworks display. I hope you can forgive me."

"I find your enthusiasm extremely refreshing," Jake said, placing his arm around her shoulders. "And as for your falling over something, perhaps I can keep you steady while you indulge in your heavenly vision."

Becky threw her head into his shoulder and snuggled it there a moment while she laughed. "That might work just fine." She pointed toward one of the outbuildings. "Let's walk that way, Jake. I think I see some horses in the corral."

He strode with her toward the stable and grinned as she continued to glance from the stars above to the barn ahead of them. When they reached the corral fence, Becky continued to look from the sky to the horses.

She leaned against the fence, resting both of her hands against one of the rails. "Oh, Jake, I don't know which is more breathtaking. The animals are magnificent in the moonlight. Look how strong and beautiful they are."

He placed his hands around either side of her against the same rail of the fence. "Yes, beautiful," he said, his lips close to her ear.

"How pleasant it must be to live in the peace and quiet. I can see why you came back from the city to live here."

"I wouldn't live anywhere else."

Becky turned within the circle of space Jake's arms allowed to look up at him. "Jake—" Suddenly she screamed, and Jake reflexively pulled her to him. An intense growl had appeared from nowhere. "My gosh, it's a wolf!" Becky clutched her arms around Jake as hard as she could.

He hid his smile and squelched the laugh that pounded against the inside of his ribs. She felt too good inside his arms to tell her right away that what she heard was only his dog. "Could be, or maybe a coyote," he said in a voice that fueled her fear.

Becky pressed tighter against him. "Take me back to the house," she pleaded. "Maybe the country isn't as beautiful as I thought."

Jake couldn't hold back his laughter any longer.

"Are you crazy?" Becky pushed against him. "We're in danger! We've got to get back to the house!"

The growl came again, and in a panicked heartbeat Becky jumped back into Jake's embrace as she released another scream.

From the darkness behind them the growl sounded one more time, louder, much louder than before.

Becky pushed herself away from Jake and slapped his chest. "You can stand here and laugh at me if you want, but I'm getting out of here. I'm in no hurry to be dinner for a wolf." She turned to run.

Jake grabbed her hand and pulled her back. "Becky, calm down. It's only Blackjack."

"What?" She threw her hair out of her face.

Still holding her hand, Jake bent to pet his dog. "Blackjack, my dog. I assure you, she's quite harmless."

Becky yanked her hand away from the cowboy. "Your dog?" She playfully slapped his arm. "Why didn't you tell me? I'm going to remember that you have a mean streak in you, Jake Ruskin, and I'm going to warn the women about it."

"I guess you'll never find anyone for me now, will you?"

Becky laughed as Blackjack placed a gentle dog kiss on her fingers. "Your secret's out now," she said, smiling up at Jake. She bent to rub her fingers into the jet black fur of the part lab, part golden retriever. "Does he tease you too, Blackjack?"

The dog barked on cue, and Becky and Jake laughed together.

"She's a good dog," Jake said, taking Becky's hand and pulling her back to a standing position. "She keeps the wolves and coyotes away."

Becky slid a sly grin over her face. "I bet." She turned back to the corral, placing her hands on the rails again.

Jake stood behind her as close as before, wishing he had another opportunity to take her into his arms. Perhaps he was one kind of wolf Blackjack wouldn't keep away from Becky.

"How many horses do you have, Jake?"

"Right now, ten. Usually I have more on hand. I had to sell a couple of them, but I'll be replacing them soon."

"You use them all for herding cattle?"

"Mostly."

A gust of wind came out of the west, and Becky shivered.

Instantly, Jake removed his blazer. He turned Becky toward him and placed the jacket around her shoulders. As he held the lapels, he pulled her closer and secured her to him with his eyes. He leaned nearer to her, hungering for a taste of her sweetness.

Becky parted her lips. She stared up at him in silence. She looked as though she were suddenly under a spell, his spell.

Jake dropped the lapels and moved his hands to Becky's cheeks. He traced her mouth with his thumbs, and inched himself closer to her. The moonlight glowing all around her made her shine like an angel, and Jake felt as though he held a little bit of heaven within his hands.

Becky pulled in a deep, shaky breath as her eyes betrayed her sudden vulnerability.

Jake touched her lips again and moved nearer, ever nearer until his lips stopped mere centimeters from hers. One last look into her deep, dark eyes before he tasted her for the first time. . . .

Blackjack released a series of frenzied barks. Becky shook herself free of Jake's grasp. "Do you suppose she saw a wolf?" Becky asked, her eyes as large as Frisbees.

Jake laughed to himself and secretly agreed that perhaps she did—a human one. "I suppose she heard a raccoon or some other nocturnal varmint," he said casually as he tried to hide the frustration his loyal dog had caused with her untimely barking.

Becky pulled Jake's jacket tight around her and straightened her spine. "Nevertheless, I'm heading back to the house. The next time I want to look at the stars, I'll look out the window."

Before he could stop her, Becky was twenty paces ahead of him. Jake bent next to his dog and put his arm over the top of her. "Thanks a lot, Blackjack." The dog placed a lick right over his lips. "That's not the kiss I was hoping for, old friend."

Becky heard a commotion outside her bedroom door. She lifted her head and tried to open her eyes. Was it even morning yet? She plopped her head back into her pillow. She heard something again and futilely tried to wake herself. She'd barely returned to her dream when a knock sounded at her door.

"Miss Montoya?" Jake's deep voice sounded soft through the door. "Miss Montoya, are you awake?"

She heard his voice and tried to wake herself, but she was as sleepy as she'd be if she'd been drugged.

She heard the door creak open, but still she couldn't bring herself to full consciousness.

"Miss Montoya." Jake's husky voice was louder now, firmer.

Becky stirred and brushed at her shoulder. When her hand met with a hardened forearm, her eyes finally snapped open. She focused on the grinning face above her. "Jake?" She sat up in bed, her covers falling around her. Becky pushed her hair behind her ears. Suddenly she noticed Jake's gaze had dropped below her neckline, and she quickly gathered the sheet to cover her silky yellow negligée. "Mr. Ruskin." Becky glanced toward the window, then back at Jake. "It's morning already?"

"It is in the country," he said, raising his eyes to meet Becky's. "It's nearly five-thirty. I thought you'd like to sleep a little longer than usual, this being your first morning on the ranch."

Becky raked her fingers through her hair with one hand while she gripped the sheet with the other. "Later than usual? Are you kidding? Five-thirty is later than usual?"

Jake straightened up. "It is in the summer time. Winters we don't get up until six or six-thirty, but summers it's more likely to be four-thirty or five. There's always too much to do."

"Well, then I guess I owe you a thanks, don't I?" Becky covered a yawn. "Excuse me, I'm still waking up."

"A nice hot shower will help." Jake moved to the door. "Sam'll have breakfast ready in twenty minutes. We're going to move some cattle this morning. Wear appropriate clothing." He placed his hand on the door knob and started to close the door, but stopped short. "Miss Montoya, have you ever ridden a horse?"

Becky shook her head, loosening the long black strands she'd tucked behind her ears. "I'm afraid not."

Jake tilted his head to one side and grinned. "Well, then I guess today is your lucky day." He closed the door behind him.

Becky slid back under her covers. Lucky? No day that starts before six A.M. could possibly be lucky. To coax herself out of bed, she reminded herself that in Chicago it was an hour later. Only thirty minutes until seven there. But her little trick on herself was unconvincing. If it was six-thirty in Chicago when she rose, it was after midnight when she went to bed. No matter how she figured it, she was short on sleep. And now she had to learn to ride a horse.

Staggering to the bathroom, Becky reached for the

shower knobs and turned the water on full force, steaming, inviting. She tossed the nightie aside and stepped into the hot stream. Would Jake's generous fee—the money that would help her to make the expansion she'd dreamed of for years—really be worth all she'd have to go through to find him a wife?

Jake stared at his newspaper and sipped coffee waiting for Becky to come downstairs. He wasn't actually reading the paper. He was glancing at the print and ads, but he was thinking about Becky and spending the day with her. He'd enjoyed everything about their time together the day before. She fascinated and intrigued him more than anyone he'd ever met in his life. She was more beautiful than any woman he'd ever been with or wanted to be with—and he wanted to be with Becky. He wanted to be with her in every way he could. He craved a knowledge of her inside and out.

He smiled as he remembered how naturally they'd turned "Mr. Ruskin" and "Miss Montoya" into "Jake" and "Becky" the night before as they stargazed. In those few minutes under the moon, Becky seemed to belong to him and his ranch. He liked the feeling he got whenever she was near, a feeling of wholeness and completion.

Jake closed his paper and tossed it onto the coffee table. He sipped the last of his coffee. As Becky learned and studied him, he'd learn about her, as intimately as he could.

"I'm not sure if I'm awake yet," Becky called from near the top of the stairs, "but at least my eyes are open."

Jake stood and smiled, his pulse quickening at the

sight of her. She'd been tempting enough to devour half-asleep and half-clothed in the sexy nightgown he'd seen her in earlier. Covering herself in snug jeans and an equally form-fitting lime-green T-shirt did little to hide what the scanty negligée had revealed. "You'll be fine after one of Sam's breakfasts."

Now at the bottom of stairs and standing next to Jake, Becky lifted a confrontational hand. "Oh, I eat only yogurt and coffee for breakfast."

A chuckle rattled Jake's ribs. "Not this morning, Miss Montoya. You aren't going to be sitting in an air-conditioned office ahead of a computer. You're going to be straddling a horse and discovering muscles you didn't know you had. You'll need a substantial breakfast, and Sam will see to it that you get one."

Becky opened her mouth to protest, but stopped when Jake pressed a finger to her lips. She softened her stance. "You're the boss, but if I put on ten pounds while I'm here, it'll be your fault."

"Put on ten pounds?" Jake asked, lifting his brows. "Ten more pounds would only enhance your beauty, Miss Montoya, but I'm afraid with what I have planned for the week, you'll be lucky if you don't lose ten pounds."

Jake watched in amusement as Sam coaxed Becky to eat all of the steak and eggs he'd set before her, then insisted she have a fresh-baked caramel roll before he'd let her leave the table. Knowing the habits of lady executives from his stint in New York, Jake silently wagered that Becky had eaten more in that one breakfast than she normally ate in a whole day on the job in Chicago. As he let his gaze run the length of her when she stood from the table, he decided she'd look real good with a few more pounds on her slender body, but he knew she'd never gain them on his ranch. He'd keep her too busy for that.

By seven, Jake had instructed Becky in the fine art of keeping herself in a saddle. She'd learned quickly as he thought she would. Sam had filled two backpacks full of the supplies they'd need for the day and given them to Jake. At exactly five minutes after seven, the delivery man arrived with Becky's new boots.

Jake showed her how to pull them on. "They're not glass slippers, but then they aren't meant for dancing."

Forty-five minutes later, Becky, Jake, and Blackjack were gathering a small herd of cattle to head north from one pasture to another with a better stand of grass. Jake told her they had to move slowly and that their ride would take most of the day. He kept the pace slower than usual so her initial experience in the saddle wouldn't tax Becky too much.

The day was an exceptional one filled with bright sun and a gentle breeze. By noon both Jake and Becky had shed their jackets and tied them to the blanket rolls on the back of their saddles.

Jake knew Becky would need a break from setting astride her mount so he purposely instructed Sam to pack a lunch that would require them to stop long enough to build a fire and cook their meal.

"Let me help you down," Jake said, quickly dismounting Scout and stepping next to Becky. He reached up to circle her waist with his hands.

Becky rested her hands on his shoulders as she gratefully accepted his help. "Whew," she breathed when her feet touched the ground, "staying on a horse is a lot harder than it looks."

"That's because you're not used to it yet." Jake reluctantly let go of her mid-section. He tilted back his Stetson. "It helps if you let yourself relax and move with the horse." He patted the animal's rump. "Cactus is real dependable."

Becky pulled the seed cap from her head and let her locks fall around her shoulders. "I'll remember that," she said, tossing her hair over her shoulders.

"I've got some wood there near that tree," Jake said, pointing. "I'm going to build a fire and make some lunch. Would you mind taking Blackjack over that rise to let her drink from the creek?"

"I'd love to," Becky said, fluffing Blackjack's furry head. "My legs could use a little stretching."

Jake took a large canteen from the side of his horse. "You could fill this with water so we can wash up."

Becky took the canteen and told Blackjack to follow her. "Be right back," she called to Jake.

Jake watched her move over the land with the grace of a gazelle. He wiped his finger over his upper lip. *The last thing those long legs need is stretching*, he thought wickedly. He shook his head and turned his attention to other flammable matters.

Before Becky reached the campsite Jake had built seemingly out of nothing, she could smell the scent of frying bacon. It set her to salivating. She couldn't believe she was hungry again—and for more meat. Steak for dinner, again for breakfast and now bacon for lunch. She was definitely going to gain ten pounds. She stopped and patted Blackjack's head. "I guess if I get fat, I'll have enough money from this job to go to a spa and trim down again, won't I, Blackjack?"

The peppy dog responded by licking her hand.

Becky quickly covered the last fifty feet to the

campfire. "I hope you don't mind," she said to Jake. "Blackjack decided to take a bath while she had a drink."

"You stinky wet dog," Jake scolded. "Shame on you. You're going to have to lie by the horses so you don't smell up our meal."

"Sorry, Blackjack," Becky said, foolishly thinking the dog's feelings might actually be hurt. She turned to Jake and shrugged. "I really didn't know how to keep her out of the water."

"When she's doing something she shouldn't or something you don't want her to do, just tell her 'no, Blackjack.' She obeys pretty well. But I don't care if she jumps in the creek, and she doesn't mind lying by the horses. So no harm done." Jake piled two tin plates with bacon, biscuits, slabs of cake and slices of apples. He poured fresh, hot coffee into two tin cups. He set the meal on the blanket he'd laid on the ground.

"It looks great," Becky said, seating herself near one of the plates. "I didn't think I'd be hungry for days after that huge breakfast, but I'm starved. Must be the fresh air."

"And the exercise," Jake said, sitting next to her.

"Exercise? All we've been doing is sitting."

He couldn't hold back the giggle her naiveté forced from him. "You mean you don't feel like you've done anything?"

Becky bit a piece of bacon and innocently shook her head.

"You will, Miss Montoya, you will."

About five that afternoon, Becky remembered what Jake had said about feeling the pains of sitting in the saddle. The man knew what he was talking about. She ached all over. "How much farther, Jake?"

"We're almost there." He pointed to the horizon ahead of them. "Do you see that shack?"

Becky shaded her eyes and peered ahead. "Yes."

"The meadow is just beyond it."

She released a sigh of relief and nodded. "Do you suppose we can stop at the shack and rest a while?"

Jake scrutinized the horizon to the west. "I think we won't have a choice. Those clouds will be on top of us before we know it. We may even get rained on before we reach the cabin."

Becky inspected the clouds herself. She shook her head. "I doubt it. They look a lot farther away than the cabin does."

"We'll see," Jake said. "One thing's for sure, though. We won't make it back to the ranch tonight." He rode away from her and yelled at Blackjack as a few of the cattle began to wander away.

Becky felt the last of her energy drifting from her aching body. Why weren't they at the shack yet? It hadn't looked that far away when Jake had pointed it out. She surveyed the sky and began to change her mind about being able to reach the cabin before the rain hit.

The downpour struck suddenly and fiercely. Becky was immediately drenched. The cattle picked up their pace, and Jake and Blackjack guided them the remaining few hundred yards to the pasture.

Becky reached the shack the same time Jake did. They tucked the horses and Blackjack safely inside the lean-to on the side of the shack and went into the cabin.

"Look at me! I'm drenched!" Becky laughed as she tugged at her wet hair.

She really didn't have to tell him to look at her. He didn't take his eyes from her. "I'm sorry, Miss Montoya. We're going to have to get out of these wet things."

Chapter Four

"There should be a change of clothes or two in here," Jake said as he walked to a tiny closet tucked next to the fireplace. He reached inside and pulled out a pair of jeans and a flannel shirt, a belt and a pair of men's boots. He held up the cache of extras and turned to Becky. "Sorry, this is all that's here." A naughty grin swept his face. "Which do you want, the shirt or the pants?"

"Ha, ha," Becky said flatly as she reached for the green plaid flannel shirt. "Where can I change?"

"Unless you want to get wet again, you'll have to change right here, Miss Montoya. It's a one-room cabin."

Becky glanced around—fifteen by twenty, a bed, a tiny sofa, a braided rug in front of the fireplace over a plank floor, and a sink with a pump, one cabinet above it and one below. She reached toward Jake. "I'll take the belt too." She thrust her eyes up to meet his gaze. "I hope I can trust you to give me a little privacy in that corner over there," she said, pointing.

Jake bowed gracefully. Then he cocked his head and smirked. "I hope I can trust you to do the same."

Becky raised a brow. "A mean streak and a sense of humor. I'll remember them both for your profile."

Jake chuckled and kept his eyes on her as she crossed the room. When she began to disrobe, he reluctantly turned away and slipped out of his own wet clothes and into fresh jeans. He hung his dripping garments over a bench near the fireplace and started to build a blaze. Before he'd brought the fire to life, Becky's clothes joined his.

As Jake squatted at the hearth, he felt Becky standing next to him. He turned his eyes toward her. They traveled up the long, bare legs slowly before sliding over the belted flannel shirt and settling on her dark gaze. "The fire will be ready in a minute," he said over the tightness in his throat. He swallowed against a growing constriction. "If you'll look in those two cabinets, you should find some canned food and some cookware we can use over the fire."

Becky went straight to the cupboard to do as Jake had suggested. The cowboy turned back to the fire. Beads of perspiration dampened his forehead though the fire had barely sparked. His arms froze in the sudden cold air the storm brought with it, but heat rose within him. He briefly glanced toward Becky as she bent to take something from the lower cabinet. Looking back at the fire, he decided there was no way he was going to be able to control his desire for the beautiful matchmaker in such close quarters.

Jake finished with the fire. He sat on the tiny sofa and slid into the extra pair of boots. He pulled a rain slicker from the small closet. "I'm going out to the lean-to to feed and water the horses and Blackjack."

He reached for the bucket next to the sink and filled it with water from the pump.

Becky folded her arms and leaned against the small counter next to them. "Can I help?"

Jake pushed his eyes toward the swirling water in the bucket and shook his head. "No. I won't be long." He cleared his throat and risked a glance in Becky's direction. "What did you find us to eat?"

Becky read the labels on the cans she found as she held them for Jake to see. "Green beans, beef stew and peaches. And, luckily, we have a can opener. But there's only one pot."

"No problem. I'll put the beans in with the stew. I'll heat them when I get back from feeding the animals." Jake took the full bucket and hastened out the door.

When he returned some time later, Becky was at the hearth warming their dinner. "It's almost ready," she said, turning from her perch when she heard the door close.

Jake nodded toward her and hung the slicker on the nail near the door. He turned toward Becky and stared at her as she stirred their food. She was so beautiful, and the sight of her leaning over his hearth warming his meal only intensified the urges he'd tried to squelch by returning to the battering rain.

"Mr. Ruskin," Becky said, rising with the warmed pot of stew in her protected hand, "I think it would be wise for us to use this time together productively." She set the pot on the wood-planked counter and filled metal dishes with their dinner. "Perhaps you could tell me what some of your favorite things are." Becky filled two metal cups with water from the pump. She handed a cup and a plate with a fork to Jake. "Would you mind doing that?"

Her clinical voice and the use of his surname took the edge off his primal desires. "My favorite things? You mean like 'raindrops on roses and whiskers on kittens'?"

Becky chuckled at his reference to *The Sound of Music* song. "Are you trying to tell me you like musicals?" She sat on the little sofa with her plate in her lap.

"I did see a couple of Broadway shows while I lived in the Big Apple, but I wouldn't say they are among my favorite things."

Becky lifted a finger. "But I know you like cats. You must have a dozen of them running around your barn."

"Like them?" Jake shrugged. "I never thought about it. The reason I have cats is to keep the mouse population down."

Becky's eyes widened. "Mice?" She drew her legs up under her. "You have mice?"

Jake threw his head back and chuckled at her unexpected surprise. He looked back at her, still grinning. "Yes, mice, rats, skunks, snakes and all kinds of other varmints. What do you think lives in the country—only horses and people and cattle?"

Becky shuddered. "Good heavens! Do you suppose there are mice or snakes here?" She gulped and scanned the room around her.

Jake eyed her carefully without hiding his amusement. "Yes, I do."

Becky threw her plate to the floor and slid into Jake as though she'd received an electric shock. "I hate mice, snakes too."

Jake set his plate on the floor and wrapped his arms around Becky. He leaned his lips close to her ear. "If I had known I'd get this reaction from your phobias, I'd have mentioned the scary critters a lot sooner."

Becky wriggled away from him and turned toward him, fear dominating her upward gaze. "Don't tease me, Ja—, Mr. Ruskin. I really am afraid."

Jake stroked her hair gently. She wasn't kidding. "I'll tell you what. We can bring Blackjack inside. She's better at catching mice than most cats. If there's a mouse anywhere at all, she'll sniff it out and dispose of it. As for snakes, they much prefer the outdoors. You don't have to worry about them."

"You're sure?"

He touched her hair once more. "I'm sure."

When they finished their meal, Jake went to get his mouse-catching dog. By the time he returned, Becky was sound asleep, sitting up on the sofa. Jake hung his slicker and told Blackjack to lay next to the fire. Then he slipped onto the couch next to Becky. "Miss Montoya," he said softly. He slid closer, lifting a few black strands from her forehead with his fingers. "Miss Montoya."

Unable to wake her, he stared at her, studying every inch of her beautiful face as carefully as he could. He decided in that instant, as he focused on her loveliness, if he'd see Becky every day for a hundred years, he'd never get tired of looking at her. And if he knew her that long, he'd never have enough of being with her.

"Miss Montoya." He wanted to wake her and take her into his arms, feel her lips against his, explore the softness of her skin. The flames flickering in the hearth magnified her attractiveness, but they couldn't compete with the tender warmth her mere presence added to the tiny cabin, even as she slept.

"Miss Montoya." Still she didn't stir. They were alone in the intimate hideaway with no one around for miles and miles. Jake couldn't help but stare at the beautiful woman and imagine what he wanted to happen between them, what might happen right that moment if he could rouse her from her deep sleep. He was sure she didn't find him unattractive. The night before she hadn't pulled away from him when he'd come so near to kissing her. She hadn't moved a millimeter when he encased her cheeks in his palms.

She'd called him "Jake" instead of "Mr. Ruskin." He loved the way she said his name. "Miss Montoya— Becky." He tried one more time to gently wake her. When she still didn't move, his heart was touched by the exhaustion her dedication to him had brought her. He brushed his fingers over her cheek. "You poor woman. What a day you've had. No wonder you're so tired."

With a flourish he whisked her into his arms and deposited her onto the bed. He covered her and tucked her in. Then he pulled a blanket and pillow from the closet, scrunched his massive body onto the tiny sofa and cursed himself for being so noble. Any other time he'd have seduced a beautiful woman in such a confined setting quicker than a con man told a lie.

Jake glanced at the fire crackling in the fireplace, then at the sleeping temptation in the bed a few feet away. Somehow Becky Montoya was different from other beautiful women he'd known, and, as he tried to fit into his cramped quarters, he wished she weren't.

* * *

Becky awoke as the first rays of light filtered through the windows of the tiny cabin. She looked around and instantly remembered where she was—alone with Jake in the middle of a beautiful meadow. Catching sight of Jake as she surveyed her surroundings, she fixed her eyes on him. He lay cramped on the tiny sofa half naked and deadly asleep. Her gaze drifted from his handsome face to the black and gray curls that covered his well-built, mammoth chest. She watched his ribs expand and contract.

Her cheeks burned, and Becky placed her palms on them to cool them. She remembered how Jake had engulfed her with his hands her first night with him. They'd dropped the "Mr. Ruskin" and "Miss Montoya" titles as soon as they stood under the stars together. Then they were Becky and Jake, not a matchmaker and a client, just a man and a woman.

She'd wanted him to kiss her, hold her, touch her. He'd wanted it too. He hadn't tried to hide his interest in her.

Last night—Becky sighed and pulled the sheets to her chin. She had no idea how they got through last night without getting close. Each of them half-clothed, alone and vulnerable with nothing to keep them out of each other's arms but their own restraint, she'd feared—or had she hoped—they'd get much closer than they should have.

She'd tried to shield the desire beneath her eyes. She knew Jake had to be aware of her attraction to him. She'd already learned how intuitive and intelligent he was. If she hadn't fallen asleep, passed out was more like it, on that sofa—yes, she had been on the sofa. She bolted forward. Jake must have carried her to bed. The thought of her half-dressed body being pressed into that magnificent, bared, masculine chest sent heat rushing through her.

A sudden deep groan from the couch sent Becky's eyes back to Jake. She watched him raise his arms over his head. He stretched and wriggled as his eyes slowly opened. "Becky?"

"I'm awake."

Jake ransacked his fingers though his hair and rubbed his hands over his face as he sat up, swinging his legs to the floor. "I'm surprised to see you up already. It's barely light out."

"I guess when a person falls asleep before eight, she tends to rise early too." Becky threw back the covers and moved to get out of bed. "Ooh, ouch!"

Jake was next to her in two strides. "Let me help you up," he said, reaching for her hand. He pulled her to her feet. "I told you you'd discover muscles you didn't know you had."

Becky couldn't straighten up. "I was hoping you weren't right, but I was afraid you would be."

"You need to loosen up. After all, you have to get on that horse and ride back after breakfast."

Becky scowled up at him. "You're a scoundrel, Jake Ruskin, and you aren't paying me near enough for this job." She pulled her hand away from him and slowly straightened her spine. She looked around the room. "Where's the . . ."

"Facility?" he asked, raising a brow. She nodded, and he poked a thumb over his shoulder. "Out back, but you'll have to wash up in here at the pump."

When they were freshened and dressed in their dry clothes, Becky and Jake enjoyed the caramel rolls Sam had packed the day before. Jake served them along with fresh, hot coffee. A couple of hours after sunrise,

Jake had things finished, and they were ready to go back to the ranch house. Becky gingerly mounted her house with Jake's expert help, and the two of them rode side by side with Blackjack leading the way.

"Give it a minute, Miss Montoya," Jake said as he observed her obvious discomfort. "You won't be so sore once you loosen up."

"If you say so." She stared straight ahead and wondered just how far they were from Jake's place. "Will it take us all day to ride back?"

"No, not nearly that long without the cattle. We should be home before mid-afternoon."

Becky nodded. "Jake, who built that little cabin we stayed in last night, and why? It isn't big enough for anyone to live in."

"It isn't meant to be lived in, just used temporarily like we did last night." He shifted in his saddle and pushed the hat back on his head. "As for who built it, my dad and I put it up when I was about ten. He was sick of sleeping on the ground every time he had to come up here."

"I see. Did you and your dad do lots of things together?"

"We worked together, if that's what you mean. He taught me about ranching."

"No, I mean did you spend special time together, intimate time, father-and-son time."

Jake reined in his mount. "I don't mean to be rude, Miss Montoya, but I don't see how that makes any difference."

Becky patted her horse's mane. "I told you some of my questions would seem like prying, but, Mr. Ruskin, what I'm trying to find out is what kind of a father you plan to be. The female clients who consider you for a husband will want to know if you'll be a loving, caring, involved father. They won't want to raise your children single-handedly."

"Whatever my father was is irrelevant. I have every intention of being completely involved in my children's lives. I wouldn't consider anything less." He spurred his horse and resumed his trail toward home.

Becky joined him. "Good. Think about this," she said, efficiently using their time to add to his profile. "If you had a free weekend to do anything or go anywhere you wanted, what would you do?"

"Miss Montoya," Jake said, looking straight at her, "I can go anywhere or do anything I want anytime I want. I have both the means and a completely trustworthy foreman who can provide me with the time." He put out his hand and waved it toward the horizon. "This is what I want to do and where I want to be."

His discomfort and agitation at being interrogated didn't slow Becky's questions. "If you were going to take your wife on a romantic weekend, where would you take her?"

Without hesitation Jake responded. "I'd take her to the most beautiful place on earth."

"And where is that?" Becky tilted her head and shaded her eyes from the sun as she stared at him.

Jake looked straight ahead. "We just came from it."

"That shack?"

He looked at her then moved next to her, bringing both of their mounts to a halt. He reached out and tucked a strand of hair behind her ear. "You didn't find it romantic there?"

"Well, I never thought of it as . . ."

"Neither did I," he said, interrupting and sliding his fingers under her chin, "until last night."

His electric touch nearly stopped her heart. The gravity of his voice stole her breath. Becky slowly dragged her eyes from his. She pointed Cactus toward the ranch and kicked him as hard as she could. The horse bolted under her direction and nearly threw her off. She hadn't a clue how to stay astride a galloping horse. All she knew was that she had to put some distance between her and Jake. She suddenly felt much too intimate with him, and very awkward and unsure of herself.

When the realization struck that she'd put herself in danger, she began to panic. She tugged on the reins and tried to slow the animal. Her unskilled maneuvers only made matters worse. In seconds, she realized she was headed toward imminent disaster.

Becky bounced and rocked and nearly fell with every beat of the horse's hooves. She had no idea how she was managing to stay astride the driving animal, she was only grateful to remain in the saddle.

Endless moments filled with futile attempts to slow her mount brought Becky close to tears and panic. About to give up and let the animal have its way, she suddenly felt herself being pulled from the saddle. She screamed and struggled against the power that over-took her.

Promptly she found herself pressed against Jake's hardened chest, wrapped in one of his arms with her legs both resting on one side of his horse. His other hand firmly tangled in the reins, Jake slowed his horse and brought it to a stop. He seized Becky's shoulders and pinned her with ice-blue eyes. "Are you out of your mind? Why did you press your horse into a run?"

Becky opened her mouth to defend her actions, but words wouldn't come. She shook her head and stared helplessly into Jake's icy gaze. Tears trickled from the corners of her eyes.

Jake slid one hand around her back and gripped her chin with the other. He sought her mouth with his and covered her lips with a hungry kiss.

Becky pressed herself into him and circled her arms around his neck. "Jake," she said, barely able to breathe. She pulled back enough to look up at him. "Jake, you saved my life."

He slid a sly grin over his face. "I had to. I didn't want to lose my horse."

Becky pounded on his chest. "Let me go. I want to walk home. I don't want to be here with you. Let me go."

Jake took her wrists. "I'm sorry, Becky," he whispered, soothing her. He lifted her and turned her so she sat directly ahead of him in the saddle. Then he circled her with his arms and took hold of the reins. "I'll take you directly home."

Becky leaned into him. She needed his comfort and his strength. She'd never been so scared in her life—and it wasn't only the runaway horse that frightened her.

Jake tightened his arms around her. He kissed the top of her head and lowered his lips to her ear. "You're all right now, Becky. You needn't tremble so."

She turned toward him, jabbed her gaze up to meet his. He pierced her through with his intensity, held her firmly, then bent to take her lips again. For a brief moment she forgot everything—the runaway horse, the mount beneath them, the meadow around them, the birds over them, her very reason for being in Montana, the reason that forbade her from the very conduct in which she so willingly participated.

The horse's momentum stopped. Jake's hands pressed tightly into her abdomen. Becky shifted in the saddle as she tried to turn to get closer to him. She needed more of him. Reading her mind, Jake brought her around enough to better connect with her lips. He raised a hand to hold her face steady, allowing him to taste her deeply. Becky nearly lost all of herself in that union, feeling more bound with him than she'd ever felt with anyone in her thirty-eight-year existence.

If it hadn't been for Blackjack's enthusiastic chorus of barks, Becky would have lived and died in the length of that one kiss. The dog's rambunctious behavior brought all of the reality back in a flash. Becky jerked herself from Jake and brought both of her hands to the saddle horn.

Jake gently spurred his horse as he took up the reins. He turned to the dog running beside him. "You picked one heck of a time to catch up to us, Blackjack."

Becky continued to grip the saddle horn and tried to regain the breath Jake had pulled from her. He seemed to have drained all her common sense too.

She inhaled deeply, concentrated on her surroundings, studied Blackjack's movements. The trees, the wild flowers, the sky, the sun, the dog, the horse— these were reality. Jake was fantasy. He was a client, and her behavior with him was inexcusable.

"Jake."

He nuzzled the top of her head with his cheek. "Hm?"

She pulled away from him. "About what just happened." She stole a quick glance toward him, then turned back to face ahead. "I shouldn't have allowed it. I'm here on business, not for any other reason. I'm afraid I lost control after the horse frightened me so. I know that's no excuse. I hope you can forgive me."

She felt a chuckle ripple over Jake's ribs as he pressed them tightly against her back. "Forgive you? No way. I think you should lose control more often. It just might do us both some good."

Chapter Five

Jake deposited Becky at the back door of his home shortly after two. Becky was glad she didn't find Sam in the kitchen. She forced her aching body through the house and up the stairs. She needed a hot shower more than she ever needed one in her life—or a cold shower. For a moment she wasn't sure which she needed more, to nurse her throbbing muscles or cool her burning desire for her client. As she reached for the hot and cold controls over the tub, a stabbing pain in her back overruled anything her emotions might have wrought. She turned the water controls to steamy and quickly disrobed. She pushed herself under the flowing stream.

Twenty minutes and two aspirin later, Becky lay under cool sheets clad in undies and a T-shirt. In a matter of seconds, she was comatose.

Jake spent the rest of the afternoon working in the barn and meeting with his foreman about the work schedule for the remainder of the week.

As he cleaned out the stalls, he was grateful for a

job he could do in his sleep. If he'd been working on a task that required real concentration, he'd have failed miserably. He couldn't think of anything but Becky. Something had happened to him in the last two days. He'd changed in a way he never would have thought possible. His heart occupied more space inside his ribs, and his mind held less reason. It was as if Becky had somehow beguiled him, though he knew undoubtedly that she had done nothing of the kind. Still, being with Becky made everything different. The old shack he'd always hated because of the way his father pushed him while they built it turned into a romantic hideaway with Becky inside. The fire he built in the hearth there took on a warmth he'd never seen in any blaze anywhere. The entire cabin glowed simply because Becky Montoya dwelled within it.

When her horse stole her from him in a deadly rush to danger, Jake had panicked at the real possibility of losing a new light that had come to fill his life. He'd rushed to save her as though he were racing to save his own life. And when he caught her, when she was safely within his arms, he didn't want to let her go, couldn't stand the thought of ever letting her be away from of his touch.

Jake stabbed at the straw and thrust the pitchfork toward the wagon holding the soiled stall bedding.

He wanted Becky Montoya. He didn't need her to find someone else for him. Not anymore. He'd found the woman he wanted to share his life with, and he'd found the love he never dreamed he could possibly encounter. He'd found it only to lose it. Becky would no more move to his ranch and be his wife than he would move back to New York and return to Wall Street. She was city, and she'd tied herself to the single life. She'd made that perfectly clear. The best Jake could hope for were stolen moments like the one they'd shared in his saddle that afternoon. He'd savor them, memorize them, and carry them with him the rest of his life. He'd say good-bye to Becky in a few days and trust that the woman she'd find for him would be a tenth as wonderful. Then he'd live the life he was fated to live with another woman and the children he'd always wish belonged to Becky.

Becky woke several hours after she fell asleep. She finished dressing and made her way toward the familiar smell of cooked beef in the kitchen.

"Evenin', Missy," Sam greeted. "Like some supper?"

Becky stifled a yawn. "Please, Sam."

"Mr. Jake already ate, but I saved you some." He pulled a plate from the oven. "Roast beef, boiled potatoes, peas and fresh-baked biscuits." He set the plate on the table.

Becky seated herself. "I didn't think I was hungry, but I'm afraid you've tempted me again with another fabulous meal, Sam."

"Thank you, Missy. I hope you enjoy it." Sam watched Becky as she tasted her first bite.

"Delicious," she said, grinning with satisfaction.

Sam waited a moment, then opened the conversation. "You and Mr. Jake have a nice time?"

"Nice? I guess so. I'm sure the whole experience will look better tomorrow after I get the feeling back in my legs."

Sam chuckled. "First time you set a horse?"

Becky nodded and took another bite of beef.

"Well, I wouldn't count on feeling too much better

tomorrow if I were you," Sam said, turning to the counter and placing some dirty dishes in the sink to rinse.

"You wouldn't, huh? Does it take a few days to get over the joys of one's initial time in the saddle?"

Grinning, Sam turned back to her. "It ain't exactly that. Mr. Jake told me you two are going to another of his pastures tomorrow to check on a different herd. He's got me making potato salad to take along."

Becky swallowed hard, a piece of beef nearly getting stuck on its way to her stomach. "We're going out again tomorrow? All day?"

"Looks like." Sam turned back to the sink. He rinsed the dishes and put them into the dishwasher. Then he started peeling potatoes.

Becky brought her plate to the sink when she finished eating. She rinsed her dishes and put them in the dishwasher. She took several steps toward the door leading to the living room and thanked Sam for the meal.

"Missy," Sam said, turning to her, "Mr. Jake just checked on those cattle in that pasture he's taking you to tomorrow a couple of days ago. I think he wants to take you out to be alone with you again."

Becky raised a hand in protest and opened her mouth to speak, but Sam stopped her.

"I don't care what you say about the two of you bein' different. Mr. Jake likes you. He likes you a lot. I do too. I'd be real pleased to have you around here permanent. And you can't do better than Mr. Jake. He's as fine as they come."

Becky couldn't help but smile at Sam's loyalty. "You know, Sam, I think if Jake were an air conditioner you could sell him to Santa Claus."

Sam laughed heartily. "You may be right, Missy, but I think you'd have a lot more use for Mr. Jake than Santa would for any old air conditioner. Mr. Jake'd be a lot warmer too."

When heat started to fill her cheeks, Becky knew she'd met her match of wits. She turned quickly and bolted from the room. It wouldn't hurt her to find her laptop computer and start filling in Jake's file. If she was going to find him a mate, she'd better get started before Sam beat her out of a job with the next female who happened by the ranch.

She'd been working a couple of hours and hadn't noticed that it had grown dark when a knock sounded at her door.

"Miss Montoya?"

"Come in," Becky called from the little desk in the corner where she'd placed her computer.

Jake came in and sauntered to her desk. "I thought I'd tell you what's on the agenda for tomorrow."

Becky leaned back in her chair and tucked her hair behind her ears. "Sam already told me. He said we were going to another pasture to check on a different herd of cattle."

Jake nodded. "Do you feel up to another day in the outdoors?" He folded his arms and leaned against the wall next to the desk.

"I love the outdoors," Becky said, stretching side to side, "but I'm not sure my back and legs will be too pleased with me when I put them into another saddle tomorrow."

"I think they'll forgive you for this ride over the countryside. I'm planning to take my truck."

Becky's face brightened enough to pale a child's on Christmas morning. "You are?"

A chuckle simmered along Jake's ribs. "You look as though I just told you we were taking a limo—with a hot tub."

"Believe me," Becky said, rubbing the backs of her shoulders, "your pickup will seem like a Rolls Royce after two days riding a horse."

Jake darted from the wall and circled behind Becky. His fingers pushed hers aside, and he began massaging her aching muscles. "How does that feel?"

"Like you have magic fingers."

"I'm sorry you're so sore. I shouldn't have taken you out on such a long ride your first day."

Becky raised her hand to cover one of Jake's. She stood and turned toward him, taking that one hand and holding it in both of hers. "I wouldn't want you to change your work schedule to accommodate me, Mr. Ruskin. Believe it or not, this isn't the first time I've had aching muscles, and it probably won't be the last."

Jake looked at his hand in hers, then raised his eyes to Becky's. "Would you mind if we dropped the 'Mr. Ruskin' and 'Miss Montoya' formalities?" He closed the small distance between them. "I think we've been much too close to be so ceremonial."

"All right, Jake." Becky dropped her eyes from his. She released his hand and turned back to her desk. "I guess I'll finish up my work. It's getting late."

Jake reached for her, turned her back to face him. "Becky."

She cleared her throat and forced her eyes up to meet the gaze she was afraid to seek. She tilted her head to one side. "Yes, Jake?"

He shifted from one foot to the other. "Becky, I . . . I, ah, I'd be glad to rub your shoulders some more if you'd like."

As she shook her head the hair she'd tucked behind her ears cascaded over her arms. "No, thanks, Jake. I'll soak in a hot tub before I turn in and take a couple of aspirin."

"Sure," he said, smiling. He reached toward her and tucked her hair back into place, resting his hands on top of her shoulders. He stared at her for a long while, and Becky feared she'd lose herself to him once again. Suddenly he dropped his hands and stuffed them into his pockets. "I'll see you in the morning."

When he turned to leave she wanted more than anything in the world to call him back. "Jake."

He took one last look at her. "Good night, Becky."

"Good night, Jake."

Becky joined Jake in the living room at nine the next morning. "Why didn't you wake me? Aren't we going to check on that herd today?"

"Good morning, sunshine," Jake said, setting his coffee on the end table and rising from his recliner. "Yes, we're still going to check on the herd, but we did have a slight change of plans. I hope you don't mind."

"Whatever you want to do is fine with me. I'm just here to tag along and observe." Becky stepped next to Jake and folded her arms.

"Good. You'd better go get something to eat from Sam and some coffee. We'll be leaving in about ten minutes."

Becky went to the kitchen where Sam fed her caramel rolls and scrambled eggs. She was about to indulge in a rare second cup of coffee when she heard the front door slam. She bolted from her seat and stepped quickly to the living room.

"Yahoo!" a little boy screamed, running to Jake. "Hiya, Jake."

Jake scooped the child into his arms. "Jimmy! How're you doing? Are your folks outside?"

The boy vigorously shook his head. "They said to tell you they'd be back at three to pick me up."

Becky had joined the duo by this time.

Jake turned to her and took her arm. "Jimmy, this is Miss Becky. Becky, this little varmint is Jimmy Holister. Jimmy's going along with us today while his dad takes his mother into Miles City."

"He is?" Becky asked brightly. "How did we get so lucky?"

"You like little boys, Miss Becky?"

"I think little boys are just terrific." She reached up and fluffed Jimmy's curly, red hair.

Jimmy took Jake's face in his tiny hands. "Jake. Jake, quit looking at her a minute. Look at me. I want to ask you something."

Jake faced the child in his arms, focusing on his sky-blue eyes. "Shoot, partner."

Jimmy lowered his voice to a whisper. "Jake, just because we have a girl along don't mean we can't still play ball and fish, does it?"

"No, partner. We'll still do everything I promised you."

"And you're going to ride us in that new rig?"

"Just like I promised."

Jimmy threw himself back. "Yahoo!" He pushed his way out of Jake's arms. "I'll go get my stuff, Jake. I left it on the porch."

"Jimmy, leave it there. I'll come around front and pick up you and your things." He turned to Becky.

"You can wait on the porch with Jimmy. I'll be with you in a minute."

Before Jake could reach the back door, Jimmy had Becky's hand and was pulling her out the front door. Eyeing Jimmy's porch stash, Becky decided this was what a seven-year-old boy would carry in his pockets if they were the size of a foot locker. Fishing gear, a baseball bat, balls and gloves and a kite with hundreds of yards of string lay strewn across the gray wooden floor boards.

"Are you sure you have everything you need?" Becky asked.

"Not everything," Jimmy said, stuffing his hands into the pockets of his overalls. "Jake's bringing the food. I get real hungry when I go with Jake." The child's eyes suddenly darted away from Becky. "Here he comes."

Becky stood and looked in the direction Jimmy pointed. "What on earth . . ." She'd seen them in the movies dozens of times, but she never imagined she'd be riding in a horse-drawn buggy. She watched Jake pull up in front of the house, dismount, and walk up to the porch.

"I hope you don't mind the change of transportation," he said to Becky, poking a thumb over his shoulder. "I promised Jimmy the next time he came by I'd take him for a ride in the new buggy. I had an old-time livery man and blacksmith build it for me."

Jimmy snapped his sky blue eyes up to Becky. "And I get to be the first rider in it." He scratched through the red curls on his head. "You won't try to race me to see who of us gets on first, will you Miss Becky? Jake did promise me, but I have to load all this stuff first."

"I'll let you be first. I'm sure Jake wants it that way."

The boy smiled gratefully, then took a load of his things to the buggy.

As the child completed filling the carriage with his gear, Jake stepped next to Becky. "Are you sure it's all right that Jimmy's coming along with us and that we're riding in the buggy?" he asked, bending close to her ear.

Becky tugged at the neck of her T-shirt as she leaned toward Jake. "It's fine, Jake, really."

"I hadn't intended this, but when his parents called, I couldn't turn them down. Jimmy's mother is expecting, and she needs to see a specialist in Miles City. They're pretty upset that she may be having some kind of complications, and they didn't want to take Jimmy along."

Becky smiled up at Jake as she learned yet another part of him. "So he's soft-hearted and a good neighbor too, huh?"

Jake straightened his spine. "I think Jimmy's ready. Let's go," he said, placing his hand on Becky's waist. He walked her to the buggy, then lifted her to her seat. Seating himself, he moved the reins and the horse hitched to the carriage began to lead while the saddled mount tied to the back followed.

Jake and Becky sat up front. Jimmy sat in the seat behind them. "This is awesome, Jake," the boy said, patting the cowboy's back.

Once they left the yard, Jake headed the wagon in a different direction than they had taken on their last outing. The terrain boasted rolling hills with a smooth trail for them to follow. Wild flowers in a palette of pastels dotted the countryside and an occasional cluster of trees broke the seemingly endless horizon. The magnificent surroundings delighted Becky almost as much as the night sky had on her first day in Montana.

Looking ahead, Becky suddenly noticed a deeper slope to the land and a large collection of trees. "What's that?" she asked Jake, pointing.

"There's a river up ahead. We're going to stop there. We'll set up a campsite. After lunch, when I've got Jimmy played out enough to get him to sit still in the saddle, I'll take him on horseback to check on the herd."

Becky leaned close to Jake. "Of the two of you, I wouldn't count on Jimmy being the one who gets played out. He's as active as a whole hive of bees."

Jake spoke softly to her. "You noticed, huh?" He turned the buggy toward the river.

It didn't take long to set up a site under an ancient oak tree. It took even less time for Jimmy to start pestering Jake to take him fishing.

"You'll have to wait, Jimmy. I've got to water the horses first and find them a place to graze."

"I'll take Jimmy fishing," Becky said.

Jake's head snapped to attention. "You know how to fish?"

Becky laughed at the shock on the cowboy's face. "What are you so surprised about? I do live by one of the biggest lakes in the world. I go fishing all the time."

"Then that settles it," Jimmy said, grabbing Becky's hand. "Miss Becky is taking me fishing, and she can use your rod and reel, right, Jake?"

"Absolutely," Jake said, waving his hand toward the river. "Don't either of you fall in."

"If we do, Blackjack can pull us out." Jimmy

pointed toward the direction from which they had come. Blackjack was on an all-out run to catch up with them.

Jake shook his head. He thought he'd left Blackjack home. Some help she'd be fishing a woman or a kid out of the water. She'd just jump in and try to play with them. Jake called Blackjack to him when the dog reached the campsite. She followed him while he freed the horses from their reins and led them to the river to drink. Though Blackjack wanted to go for a swim, Jake sternly ordered her not to. She obeyed.

When the horses were adequately watered, Jake found a place for them to graze and staked them out. Then he went to the buggy to place the lunch they'd brought on the blanket under the shade of the oak. He sat on the ground with Blackjack at his side and watched Becky and Jimmy fish.

She'd amazed him once more. Becky was indeed quite an expert fisherman. She was completely at ease handling her gear. She even helped Jimmy to improve his cast. When Jake saw the duo start to haul in some fish, he hastily put together a fire. Jimmy would want to eat his catch for lunch. Even cold hamburgers, the boy's favorite food, would take a backseat to fresh pan-fried fish.

When they'd caught all the fish they could eat, Becky and Jimmy cleaned them and Jake put them on the fire to cook. They feasted on nature's bounty along with potato salad, fresh strawberries, homemade biscuits and honey, and ice-cold cans of soda.

They'd barely finished chewing when Jimmy leaped to his feet. "Your turn now, Jake. Let's play catch." Jimmy quickly turned to Becky. "Sorry, Miss Becky,

I didn't mean to leave you out. Do you want to play ball with us?"

"I'll tell you what. You go warm up in the bull pen while I clear away the mess we made with our picnic," Becky said, sliding to her knees. "I've never played baseball before, but I'd sure like to try."

"You never played?" Jimmy's brows flew to his hairline. "How did you get to be so old without ever playing baseball?"

Jake slammed his hat on his head and lifted Jimmy under the arms. "Come on, boy, let's get you and your big mouth over to the pitcher's mound."

Becky giggled as she watched the boys stroll away. She sat back on her ankles. It was easy to see Jake would be a good father. He was great with Jimmy. In the same instant she realized Jake's capabilities, she realized her own. Despite the fact that she had spent almost no time around children, she'd handled her time with Jimmy well too. Thinking about it, she found herself truly amazed that she felt so comfortable with the child. For the first time in her life, she questioned her vow to avoid motherhood, and she began to wonder if perhaps she would be missing out on something positively wonderful.

She allowed the domestic fantasy to continue a moment longer before she sternly scolded herself. "It's too late for that now." She quickly finished tidying up the area and went to join the boys in a game of baseball.

Chapter Six

Jimmy pitched. Becky tried to hit. She'd been to hundreds of Cubs games. Hitting a ball didn't look all that difficult, but it seemed it must have been easier for the Egyptians to build the pyramids than for her to connect with a ball.

"Jake!" Jimmy yelled. "Go help her. We'll be here all day waiting for her to hit the ball."

Lowering her bat as Jake approached, Becky said, "I don't know what's wrong with me. I'm not usually so inept."

Jake came up behind her. "It's the way you're holding the bat. Try this." He placed his arms around her and helped her hold the bat. "Okay, Jimmy," he yelled.

The ball came across the makeshift plate. Jake and Becky swung and nearly made contact.

Jake raised his left hand. "Wait a minute, Jimmy." Then to Becky he whispered close to her ear. "Move with me." He placed his arms around her, his hands on hers and together they swung the bat over and over. "Feel that?"

72

All she could feel was his electrical encasement of her. "What?"

"The way to move your body. You've got to put your whole body into the swing." They swung again together. "Jimmy, throw another one."

Jimmy threw. Becky missed. Jake backed off.

"Try it without me," Jake said, "but move your whole body, and keep your eye on the ball." Jake waved his arm toward Jimmy and the boy threw the ball.

Becky made contact and the ball flew fifty feet. She instantly dropped the bat and ran to Jake. While Jimmy went after the ball, Becky threw her arms around her teacher and placed a grateful kiss on his lips. "You're something else, Jake Ruskin. Where did you learn to teach like that?" She didn't give him a chance to react. She let go of him immediately and went to pick up the bat. "Pitch me another one," she yelled as Jimmy went back to the mound. She hit the ball again.

As Jake trotted past Jimmy to the outfield, the boy asked, "What did you teach her, Jake? She's really hitting them now."

When each of the trio had his or her turn at all three positions, Jimmy decided he'd like to fly his kite. Jake helped him get started, then went to join Becky on their picnic blanket. She was lying on her side, her elbow resting on the blanket, her head on her hand. Jake lay down next to her, then perched up on his elbows so he could watch Jimmy.

"He's quite a kid," Becky said as Jake made himself comfortable on the blanket.

Jake took off his hat and raked his fingers through his hair. "He's all boy, that's for sure."

"You're good with him, Jake. You're going to make a great father."

"I think so too," he said, allowing a grin to cover his face. He reached for a strand of hair that lay over Becky's forehead. "You looked like a natural yourself, Becky."

She shrugged. "Jimmy's easy to be around."

"It isn't just that." Jake glanced in Jimmy's direction to make sure the boy was all right, then turned on his side to face Becky. "You've got wonderful instincts. You should rethink your position on not becoming a mother."

Becky shook her head. "No, it's too late for me. I'm not twenty-five anymore."

"Aren't you?" Jake smoothed his hand over her hair. "You don't look a day past twenty-five to me." His eyes drifted over her face. He touched his fingers to her lips. "You're so beautiful."

Becky reached her palm to his cheek, let it rest there a brief moment, then circled her hand to the back of his neck. She lay flat on the blanket and pressed Jake closer to her.

He hovered above her, his eyes fixed on hers. His fingers traced her lips and her cheek. Slowly they slid down her neck until his hand came to rest beside her head. He inched his way toward her, joining his lips to hers.

Becky laced her fingers through his thick hair. She called his name when his lips left hers in search of her forehead, her eyes, and her jawline before he captured her mouth again. His lips toyed with hers, teased her, tantalized her with a long, lingering touch of their flesh.

Jake pulled back, and Becky arched toward him until she caught his lips once more. He wrapped his arm around her and lowered her back to the ground.

Becky let herself feel loved and wanted and cherished. She allowed her heart to soar as Jake touched her with the greatest of care and the utmost in tenderness.

From nowhere a pang of guilt stabbed at her. She suddenly pushed Jake away and stood. She stepped toward the trunk of the great oak above them. She turned and leaned her back into it.

Jake sprang to his feet. He went to her and placed his hands on either side of her, his closeness pinning her to the wood. He bore through her with his eyes.

Becky parted her lips. She tried to speak.

"You're beautiful, Becky, inside and out. I could spend an eternity with you and never grow tired of gazing into your eyes."

Becky slowly turned her head from side to side.

Jake caught her jaw, steadied her, took her lips gently.

Becky didn't want to be reasonable, she wanted to be cherished—and, oh, how Jake made her feel cherished. She leaned into him, melded with him, traced the taut muscles of his back with her slender fingers. She wanted him to kiss her like this every day of her life.

When Jake pulled away enough to look into her eyes, she wanted him back at once. She hadn't had nearly enough of him. She wanted to say "Don't stop," but he'd stolen nearly all the breath from her body. She parted her lips. "Jake, don't . . ." She had only enough air to utter two words.

Jake quickly dropped his arms and turned away from her. He dragged his fingers through his hair, then whirled back to her. "I shouldn't have done that. You made it clear to me yesterday that you wanted to keep our relationship strictly professional." He lifted her chin with his fingers. "I'm sorry."

Becky shook her head as Jake dropped his hand. She had to explain what she meant to say, but she wasn't sure she could. "Jake, I didn't . . ."

"You don't have to say anything, Becky. I know the score. You have your life, and I have mine. We're on two different paths." He took her face into his hands and smiled down at her. "But I'm glad our paths crossed even for a little while." He kissed her lightly, then walked away.

He returned in a few minutes with Jimmy and a broken kite. Jake told Becky he and Jimmy were riding to check on the herd, then he'd take her back to the ranch.

Becky sat on the blanket and watched Jake and Jimmy ride away. She could use the time alone to straighten out the mass of confusion ransacking her mind.

She laced her fingers through her hair and tightened them against her scalp. "Oh, Jake Ruskin, why have you made everything so complicated?" Becky glanced toward the cowboy astride his mount clutching the child ahead of him. They grew farther and farther away from her physically, but Jake wasn't far away from her at all. He occupied his own place in her heart; she breathed him as she inhaled his ranch air.

As though gingerly opening and peering through a forbidden door, Becky carefully, slowly allowed herself to imagine the impossible—a life with Jake. She sat and drew her knees up and placed her forehead against them. She saw their names on the mailbox.

Jake and Becky Ruskin. She imagined a baby boy being held by the proudest father on the planet. She listened for the voice of a toddler calling her "Mama." She dreamed of being with Jake in the little cabin, alone and warm, entwined in each other's arms, their hearts beating in unison, their lips hungrily seeking, their touches learning and gently exploring.

A ringing phone intruded, an e-mail notification sounded, her secretary told her her next appointment had arrived.

Becky shook her head. "No." She shivered. How could she even pretend to put her life in Chicago behind her? She'd spent over fifteen years building everything she had out of nothing but an idea. She was a career woman through and through. She wasn't a mother or a wife. That was for her clients, not for her. She'd never seen herself in that blessed vocation before. It couldn't possibly be beckoning her now.

She quickly cleared the campsite and extinguished the fire where they'd cooked the fish. As she kicked dirt over the last of the embers, she wished she could smother the burning flames Jake ignited within her as easily.

Becky fished away the rest of the time she waited for Jake and Jimmy to return. Catching and releasing filled her thoughts with something other than what she could not have.

The ride back to the ranch was quiet. Jimmy dozed in his seat and slept over the bumps of the prairie. Jake sat close to Becky and stared straight ahead as he guided the horse home.

When they reached the farmyard, Jake woke Jimmy and told him to get a piece of cherry pie from Sam before his parents arrived. Jake didn't have to suggest the pie twice. Jimmy reached the back door before Jake had helped Becky out of the carriage.

"I guess he likes cherry pie," Becky said, placing her hands on Jake's strong shoulders as he lifted her to the ground.

"About like a lazy man loves a recliner on a porch." Jake grinned down at Becky and touched his finger to her chin. Abruptly he turned to the horse hitched to the buggy and released it from its harness. He led the animal around the back of the rig and untethered the other mount.

"Could I take one of the horses for you?" Becky asked, reaching for a strand of leather.

Jake handed her a lead.

A moment later they were alone in the barn, Jake tending the horses, Becky watching in silence. She leaned against a rail around the stall where Jake put one of the mounts. "You truly belong here, Jake. I've never seen anyone so natural in his environment."

He opened and closed the gate of the stall and moved beside her. He leaned against the rails and pushed back his hat. He removed his gloves and stuffed them into his back pocket. "I didn't always think so." He dropped his eyes, then raised them back to Becky. "When I turned eighteen, I couldn't wait to get out of here. I hated the ranch. All I wanted was to put myself through college and make a fortune. I didn't care if I ever saw a ranch, a horse, a prairie or cattle again." He removed his hat and placed it on a post. His lips curved slightly upwards. "You probably won't believe this, but I liked living in New York. I most likely would have stayed there if Pop hadn't left me the ranch, such as it was back then. In fact, as I told you,

I had intended to sell it and head right back to the Big Apple."

"You really liked city life?"

Jake gave her a crooked nod. "I did, but when I came back to the ranch, something happened to me. I found something I didn't even know I'd lost. I found myself," he said, looking around before returning his eyes to Becky's, "in all of this. That kind of connection can't really be explained. It's something a person has to experience for himself. What I can tell you, though, is that I've never felt anything as powerful as that in my life . . ." He slid his fingers under Becky's chin. "Until now."

Becky pulled away from the static of his touch. "Jake, don't say that."

He reached for her, pulled her close, bit into her with his eyes. "It can never be wrong to care for someone, Becky, not the way I care for you."

She struggled against her heart as she did against him. "Yes, it can be wrong, Jake, when two people are wrong for each other. Caring for the wrong person can only lead to misery and heartbreak."

"How can you be so sure we're not right for each other?" He seized her shoulders. "I didn't mistake the way you felt in my arms, Becky. You're not blind to it either. We're like a volcano about to erupt when we're together. We owe it to ourselves to see where these feelings lead us."

Becky fought the liquefying effect his words had on her heart and her strength. She stiffened her limbs and her spine and dragged herself away from him. She raised her chin defiantly. "I came here to do a job for you, Jake. I've been completely out of line in my behavior when we've been alone. I should turn around and walk, no, run back to Chicago. I've behaved despicably." She stalked toward the door of the barn.

Jake caught her shoulder and spun her around. "No way, lady. You're not going anywhere."

He didn't put his hands on her this time. He didn't need too. His icy gaze pinned her where she stood.

"You couldn't do anything despicable if you tried, and the last thing you should do is chastise yourself for acting like a woman." Jake touched his hand high on Becky's ribs. "I think that you discovered for the first time that you have a heart as vulnerable and empty as the women who come to you looking for their special man." He drew his hand back. "There's nothing in the world wrong with that."

Becky looked down and kicked at a clump of straw. She raised her eyes back to him. "You're wrong, Jake." She spun away from him before he could read the truth in her eyes, before she unwittingly affirmed everything he'd said.

Jake captured her once more before she reached the door. He held her arms from behind her and bent low to her ear. "You can't just walk away from what we could have, what neither of us ever believed we'd have a chance to find. You can't throw away something that rare and precious."

Becky would have collapsed in that instant if he hadn't been holding her arms so tightly. "Jake," she said, hoping she'd be able to summon the strength she needed so desperately, "There's nothing to throw away. You've got to believe that." She didn't turn to look at him. She'd have been lost for sure if she had.

Jake let go of her.

Becky immediately moved away from him, putting one foot in front of the other, aiming herself toward the back door of the house. Before she reached her target, Jake neared her.

"Becky, wait."

She stopped and turned to look up at him.

Jake touched her cheek with the backs of his fingers. "Are you sure?"

"Sure?"

"About us."

"Jake, that's just it. There is no us. There's only you and me, and we're not together. We never could be."

In the time it takes for a light to flash, Jake swept Becky into his arms and kissed her with every drop of the intensity he felt for her. He took his time, savoring her, memorizing everything about her. If this was good-bye, he was going to make it one to remember. When he'd taken and given all the moment allowed, he pulled back enough to look into her blazing dark eyes. "If you ever change your mind, I'll be here." He released her just as Sam opened the back door.

"Mr. Jake, Jimmy's folks already came to pick him up, but Lucas Rolland is here to see you. I told him you was busy. I can send him away if you want." Sam looked from Jake to Becky and back to Jake again.

"I'll see him, Sam. Tell him we'll be right in." Jake turned back to Becky. "Are you okay?"

She nodded slowly, then lifted her chin. "I'm fine," she said, trying to appear nonchalant. She turned to go up the two steps leading to the back door and stumbled on the first stair.

Jake chuckled as he caught her. Whether she wanted to admit it or not, she was no more fine after that kiss than he was. Maybe sometime before she left she'd admit it.

Jake washed his hands at the sink, then took Becky into the living room to meet Lucas Rolland.

As they entered the room, six-feet, two-inches of blond cowboy rose from the sofa and turned to meet them. "Wow!" Lucas exclaimed, eyeing Becky. "Who's the pretty filly, Jake? Have you been holding out on me?"

"Cool it, cowboy," Jake possessively said in his husky voice. "This is Becky Montoya. She's visiting from Chicago."

Becky put her hand forward and Lucas clutched it tightly, pulling her toward him. "Glad to know you, Mr. Rolland."

"Not half as glad as I am to know you, Miss Montoya," he said, his deep, navy blue eyes scanning her snug-fitting gray T-shirt and jeans. "Where are you from?"

"Chicago." Becky tilted her head and smiled.

"Married, are you?" asked the blond cowboy.

"No, Mr. Rolland, but I am a mess," she said, looking at her clothes. "If you'll excuse me," she said, tugging her hand away from Lucas, "I'll go upstairs and freshen up."

"Wait just a minute," Lucas said, stepping toward her as she turned from him.

Becky spun back to face Lucas.

"You got plans for tonight?"

She threw a questioning look in Jake's direction. He lifted his shoulders. She glanced back at Lucas. "I guess not."

"How about going to a picture show with me?"

"There's a movie theater nearby?"

"Twenty miles," Lucas said.

Becky glanced toward Jake one more time. His jaw was locked tight, and his arms were fastened over his chest as though he were holding them to keep them from flailing about. Luke's invitation out was just what Becky needed to convince Jake that there was nothing between the two of them. Becky charmed Lucas with a smile and agreed to accompany him to the movies.

"I'll pick you up at five-thirty. We'll get a bite to eat first, okay?"

Becky nodded and swung a mop of hair over her shoulder. "See you then."

Jake stared at Becky until she disappeared at the top of the stairs.

Lucas stood next to him. "You don't mind me taking out your *friend*, do you, Jake?"

"If she can stand it, I guess I can." Jake hoped his attempt at humor hid the fact that he wanted to take Lucas apart right there in his living room. He wondered momentarily if he should warn Becky about his best friend's reputation with the ladies.

Lucas glanced at his watch. "We'd better get down to business since I got myself a date in a couple of hours." He shifted from one foot to the other and folded his arms. "I've come to offer you three of the best horses in Montana, Jake. Are you ready to buy yet?"

Jake placed his hand over Luke's back. "That all depends, old friend. How bad are you intending to rob me?"

Lucas looked up the staircase, then back at Jake. "I'd say you caught me on a good day, Jake. All of a sudden, I'm feeling real generous and real grateful to you." He glanced towards the stairs again. "I just might be able to make you the best offer you ever had."

Chapter Seven

Becky saw very little of Jake over the next several days. She caught up with him to ask the few questions she needed answered for her profile, but otherwise she had no contact with him. Becky used the time to catch up on business, complete Jake's file, and locate prospective brides.

She searched her database for several women who might pair nicely with Jake. She turned up three. Each woman had expressed an interest in living in the country, especially in the West. Each was in her thirties, but every one of them was as varied in appearance as Jake's original physical description in the interview Becky had conducted in his office that first day.

Becky sent a photograph of Jake to the three women by e-mail along with his profile and his postal and e-mail addresses. Within two days she heard from two of the ladies, each expressing an interest in corresponding with him. Once she received the positive replies, Becky used Jake's printer to print out pictures of the women who responded along with their profiles and addresses and left them on Jake's desk. On top of the ladies' bios, Becky left a note:

Jake,
   My work here is finished. I'll be leaving to-morrow.
Becky.

Lucas came to pick up Becky for dinner in the evening. Becky dressed in the best she brought, a slender black dress, dark stockings, and pumps. She wore a string of pearls around her neck to match the ones in her ears. Lucas made no attempt to hide his delight when he gazed at Becky as she stood in the doorway to welcome him.

"The sunset should hide in shame tonight." He bent to kiss her cheek. "You look too good to go to any of the places around here. What am I going to do with you?"

In a single heartbeat, Lucas had taken her in his arms and melted his lips against hers. While Becky enjoyed him very much, he didn't ignite her the way Jake had.

Lucas pulled back and gazed down at her. He lifted her hair over her shoulders. "Well, young lady, since you look too good for any of the restaurants in the state, I'll tell you what I'm going to do. I'm going to take you to my place, and Mrs. Foster, my cook, is going to serve us the best meal in Montana."

Becky lifted a shoulder. "Sounds great. Let's go."

Throughout the ham, the au gratin potatoes, the broccoli and the cherries jubilee, Becky only half-listened to what Lucas said. She could scarcely believe she'd be leaving the next day. She'd probably never see Jake again.

She smiled and laughed with Lucas, but inside, her heart was breaking.

Sitting in the living room of a modern two-story home that would rival any in a Chicago suburb, Lucas covered his usually jovial face with a serious look. He took Becky's hand as he moved closer to her on the sofa. "What's wrong, Becky?"

Becky's eyes snapped up to meet his. "Wrong?" She looked away. "Nothing."

He turned her back towards him, took both of her hands into his. "I know we don't know each other all that well—yet, but you aren't yourself tonight. Something's troubling you." He brushed his fingers over her cheek. "Is it me? Have I offended you in some way?"

Becky smiled and shook her head.

The jovial grin returned to Luke's face. He snuggled his shoulder into hers. "Hm, then maybe I should have tried to," he said wickedly, "maybe I've been too standoffish."

Becky kissed his cheek. "You've been great, Luke. I've really enjoyed being with you, but I'm afraid tonight will be our last night together. I'm going back to Chicago tomorrow."

Lucas rid himself of the grin. He leaned to kiss her lightly. "I hope we have a snowstorm that cancels all the flights."

Becky burst into laughter. "It's June."

"There, that's the way a beautiful woman should look on her last night in Montana—happy, blissful, delighted. You're much too pretty to look as sad as you did a minute ago." Lucas touched his fingers to her hair. "Don't you want to go back to Chicago?"

"Of course, I do. I love it there."

"Then what's the problem?"

Becky pinched his cheek. "There isn't one. That's what I've been trying to tell you."

"Great," Lucas said, standing and pulling Becky to her feet. "Before you return to the Land of Lincoln, you have to let me show you our Big Sky. I guarantee you, you'll never look at the stars again in the same way." Lucas draped his arm around Becky's shoulders and led her outdoors.

Becky stared into the night sky and knew Lucas was absolutely right. The sky would never be the same again—not since she'd seen it with Jake.

Jake hadn't unclenched his jaw since he found Becky's note on top of the bios of the mail-order brides on his desk. Alone in the dark, sitting in his leather chair, he waited for her to come home from her date with Lucas.

He heard them on the porch, talking and laughing. He dug his fingernails into the soft leather. It took all his strength to keep himself glued to his chair. Ever since he'd introduced Becky to his best friend, Jake had wanted to tear Lucas apart. He couldn't stand the thought of Lucas touching her, kissing her, telling her how pretty she was. And he'd do all of those things and more. Jake knew Lucas. That's why he wanted to tear him apart.

The porch went silent only a moment before the front door opened and Becky stepped inside. Jake listened to them say their good nights before Becky closed the door. Once the door was shut, he turned on the lamp next to his chair.

Becky jumped. "Jake!" she cried, her hand flying to her heart, "You scared me!"

"Did I?" He scowled. "Sit down." He nodded toward the couch.

Becky stared at him as she stepped to the sofa. "Is something wrong?" She slowly lowered herself to a corner seat.

"Wrong? Yes, I think so." He held up her note. "You're leaving? You told me in a note?" He bolted from his chair and stepped toward the fireplace. He leaned a hand against the mantle and fixed his eyes on her. "I don't understand, Becky. I don't understand you at all."

"Understand? Jake, you aren't making any sense." Becky stood and walked to the opposite end of the stone hearth. "I've finished my job, or at least I've done all I can for now. Two of the three women I found most suited to you have already responded, expressing an interest in corresponding with you. It was their profiles I left on your desk. I haven't heard from the third one yet, but I'm sure she'll be equally enthusiastic. Any of them would make you a fine wife. If you just give it some time, I think you'll see that."

Jake punched his fist into his hand as he turned away from Becky. "You've done your job, Miss Montoya." He spun back to her, inched his way toward her. "You booted up your computer, searched your database, pulled out three women and poof!" He waved his hands in front of her. "You disappear. No looking back, no regrets. You move human beings the way I move cattle."

Becky folded her arms tight against her. She straightened her spine and firmed her jaw. "You, Mr. Ruskin, gave me a job to do. You hired me to find you a wife, a companion willing to marry you and give you children. I did what you asked, precisely what you hired me for." She paused, staring up at him. "Are you saying you have a complaint about one of the women who has shown an interest in you? Are neither of them to your liking? I can certainly look further. I always do everything I can to make sure my clients are satisfied with their service."

Jake suddenly softened his stance. He reached out and touched his fingers to Becky's cheek. "Oh, Becky," he said softly, slowly releasing a long breath. "I'm not really just any client, am I?" He cupped her face in his hands and bore into her gaze. "Am I?"

Becky stared up at him, her eyes glistening. "Oh, Jake, what do you want me to say?"

He closed the remaining space between them, slid his hands down her neck and onto her back as he held her with his eyes. "You don't have to say anything if you don't want to." He leaned toward her and pressed his lips to her forehead. He pulled back to look into her eyes so he could read what she might be hiding from him, but her lids shielded her soul. Jake leaned toward her again and kissed each of her eyes and her cheeks. He circled his lips to her ear. "You don't have to say a thing," he whispered. He trailed gentle kisses along her jaw line until he neared her lips. He pulled back one more time, saw that her eyes remained closed, then lowered himself to capture her lips.

Becky trembled under his embrace and reached her hands to his shoulders. She kneaded her fingers into his muscles, then slowly slid her fingers around his back.

Jake tightened his embrace, and Becky pressed him

closer. She was his. If only for the moment, she was his, and he made sure she knew it.

Becky pressed herself against Jake's powerful chest, nestling her soft cheek into his stubbly one. "Oh, Jake. I never meant for any of this to happen," she whispered, her voice raspy and low. "None of this should ever have happened."

Jake pulled back from her, palmed her cheeks, and penetrated her eyes. "Don't say that," he murmured, placing his thumbs over her lips. Before she could speak again, he covered her mouth with his, hoping he could kiss away any regret. No matter what happened between them, no matter how he might suffer if she ultimately left him, he'd never regret having known Becky Montoya. She'd be in his heart the rest of his life.

Becky leaned her head back as Jake's lips left hers to taste the sweetness of her graceful neck. "Jake," she gasped. "Jake."

The throaty sound of his name coming from the depths of her was more than he could stand. He lifted her into his arms and, in two strides, found himself at the sofa. He lowered her to the leather. As Becky lay along the cushions, Jake knelt next to her. He lifted her hand to his lips and reverently bestowed soft kisses on each of the knuckles.

Becky stared at him, wide-eyed and waiting.

Jake leaned over her. He touched his index finger to her forehead and traced the outline of her face. "You're the most beautiful woman I've ever seen." He lowered himself to her and took possession of her eager lips. Immediately her arms circled him, drawing him closer to her.

Becky sat up on the sofa without drawing away

from Jake. She helped him next to her. "Jake, I've got to tell you something," she said, her voice sounding as though the words could barely be spoken.

Jake stroked her hair and gazed into her eyes. "Anything, sunshine." His heart soared as he dared to hope that she may finally be ready to admit her feelings for him.

"I don't know exactly how to say it." Her words came a little easier now. She looked away from him, then back into his gaze. "I want you to know that I . . ." Becky jumped. "What was that?"

"What?" Jake asked without taking his eyes from her.

Becky looked around the room. "I heard something."

A knock sounded at the door.

"Were you expecting someone?" Becky asked Jake.

He stroked her hair again. "Only you, and now that I have you, I'm not moving one inch. Whoever is at the door can go away."

The knock sounded again.

Becky pushed away from Jake. "We can't just ignore a person at the door."

He pulled her back to him. They'd come so close. Nothing was going to interrupt them now. "Finish what you were saying," Jake said gently.

Becky slid a grin over her face. She kissed Jake's lips lightly. "After you answer the door."

Jake kissed her again. "You're not only a fox, you're foxy too." He rose, went to the door, and opened it.

A beautiful, blue-eyed blond slender woman about five and a half feet tall looked up at Jake. "Are you . . . ," she said, swallowing hard. "Is Becky Montoya here?"

"Becky? Yes, she is." Jake stepped aside and let the woman enter his house.

Becky bolted to her feet. "Catherine! What are you doing in Montana?"

Catherine quickly went to Becky and embraced her. "I just couldn't wait. I had to come as soon as I heard from you." She spun back toward Jake who had joined them at the sofa. Looking at Becky again, she placed a hand next to her mouth and whispered. "Aren't you going to introduce us?"

"Yes, of course," Becky said, looking from Catherine to Jake. "Jake Ruskin, this is Catherine Worthington."

Jake took Catherine's extended hand and shook it, wishing the beautiful blond would disappear. "How do you do?"

"Fine, thank you. It's a pleasure to meet you, Jake."

"My pleasure," Jake said, charm covering his face as he bowed slightly. "Are you a friend of Becky's?"

The two ladies looked at each other anxiously, then Becky turned to Jake. "Not exactly." She cleared her throat. "Ms. Worthington is one of my clients, the one who I had contacted about you who hadn't responded."

Jake felt as though his horse had thrown him. "I see."

"It's late," Becky said, nervously glancing at her watch. "Why don't we bring in Catherine's things? She can bunk with me up in my room. I saw a roll-away bed in the closet."

"Bunk with you," Jake repeated, dazed by the events of the last few moments. "Yes, Ms. Worthington, you must be tired. I'll get your things from your car."

Catherine handed her keys to Jake. "Thank you, Jake."

When Jake left the room, Catherine turned to Becky. She grabbed her and crushed her with her arms. "Oh, Becky, he's absolutely dreamy. I'll never be able to thank you enough for bringing us together. You're the most wonderful person in the world."

Becky turned away from her and pointed herself toward the staircase. "Our room is upstairs," she said, choking back tears. If only Catherine had come a few minutes later, or if she hadn't come at all, things would be so different. Everything would have been very, very different.

Catherine chattered on as she and Becky put sheets on the rollaway. Becky let Catherine ramble on about Jake and their future together while she tried to keep her heart in one piece. When the bed was finished, the hopeful bride disappeared into the bathroom, leaving Becky with orders to bring in her vanity case as soon as Jake brought it up.

She could hear Catherine singing in the shower when Jake knocked at the door. She opened the portal, and Jake stepped inside and deposited the suitcases on the floor.

Jake tossed his head toward the bathroom. "She's in the shower?"

Becky glanced at the bathroom door and nodded.

Jake touched Becky's jaw and forced her eyes to meet his. "Good. We need to finish our conversation."

Becky glanced toward the bathroom again, then back to Jake. "I think we're finished, Jake, don't you?"

He stabbed his fingers into his hair and gritted his teeth. "Why did she just show up like that? I thought we were supposed to write to each other first, talk on the phone. She wasn't supposed to just show up."

Becky grabbed at Jake's forearms as he knotted them across his chest. She squeezed them gently. "You're right. She shouldn't have just come without contacting you first. I'll tell her that, and, Jake, I can send her packing in the morning, if that's what you want."

Jake abruptly seized Becky's shoulders. "What I want is to be back in the living room before she knocked on the door. I want to be kissing you and listening to you tell me that you have feelings for me as I do for you. That's what you were going to say, Becky, isn't it? Before she . . ." Jake threw an angry arm toward the bathroom door, "Before she showed up and ruined everything."

Becky backed away from him. "Oh, Jake, is that what you thought?" she asked, letting her voice drip with sympathy. "I'm so sorry if you misunderstood me." She stepped toward him, touched his forearm, then pulled her hand back, avoiding any physical contact with him. "What I was about to say was that I'm very fond of you. I've loved every minute of being with you. I mean that. I wanted to tell you that I am going to miss you very much when I go back to Chicago. I hope your life with Catherine or one of the other women, whomever you choose, is a blessed and happy one because I think you truly deserve a wonderful woman." She touched her finger to her eye. "If I were Catherine, I'd be very happy right now at the prospect of starting a future with a man as sensational as you."

Jake shook his head. "I don't believe one word of it, but if that's the way you want it, fine." He bolted around and stepped into the hall.

"Jake, wait!" Becky called, reaching toward him.

He stopped, but he didn't turn back to her. "What is it?"

Becky touched his arm and made him look at her. "You didn't tell me what I should tell Catherine. Should I tell her to go home, or would you like her to stay?"

Jake curved one corner of his mouth upwards. "As long as she's here she might as well stay. I wouldn't want her visit here to have been a waste of time." He lifted an arm in the air. "Shoot, maybe I'll up and marry her tomorrow, then your job is done. You can collect the rest of your fee and head back to Chicago a significant few thousands richer than you were when you came."

Becky's heart fell to her toes. She'd hurt him more than she'd imagined. She could no longer stop the tears that battered her eyes. She wiped her hand over her face. "I'm sorry, Jake. I'm so sorry."

He gritted his teeth and rigidly nodded his head. "Yeah? Well I'm not." Suddenly he grabbed her and pressed an angry kiss to her lips.

Becky had none of the resistance she knew she should make evident to him. She wanted him too much.

Jake discarded the gentleness he'd used all the other times he'd kissed Becky. He plundered her lips as savagely as he'd beat a man who'd ever try to hurt her. When she went limp under his power, he knew. She wasn't lost to him yet. She didn't want to leave him any more than he wanted her to leave.

He softened his lips, gentled his hands through her hair, and she weakened even further. He knew when he released her that she could barely stand. Her eyes were wet and weak and filled with her heart. They glistened with his reflection, and he knew he was inside her. He took her lips in one brief kiss, then stepped away from her. "I'm not sorry one bit."

Becky watched him turn and pound the steps to his room. He went inside and slammed the door. She jumped at the sound of the wood hitting the jamb. She raised her fingers to her lips, swollen from his intensity as her heart was swollen with love.

"Becky."

She spun around at the sound of her name.

Catherine appeared at their bedroom door, leaning far enough into the hall for Becky to see she was draped only in a towel. "Jake's not here, is he?"

Becky nodded toward his room. "He's in there."

"Whew! I didn't want him to see me like this—not yet, anyway—but I had to get my suitcases. I need some fresh clothes."

Becky walked back into their room and closed the door. She leaned against it and absentmindedly watched Catherine take a piece of luggage into the bathroom. The thought of the intimacy Jake would share with Catherine or one of the other women cut her heart in half. She listlessly walked over to her bed, took off her clothes and slipped into her nightie. She slid into the cool sheets of the empty bed and cried for all the vacant nights which lay ahead of her. Tomorrow she would fly back to Chicago and put Jake behind her. He'd be easier to forget there, and she had to forget him. He'd soon belong to someone else.

Chapter Eight

Becky stared at the wall from her bed for a desolate eternity that actually lasted less than half an hour. The sound of her name abruptly disturbed her aching thoughts.

"Becky, could we talk a while?" Catherine asked, sitting on the edge of Becky's bed.

Becky pulled herself up to a sitting position and placed a more pleasant look on her face. "Sure."

Catherine shook her hands in front of her. "I'm not exactly sure what to say first." She rolled her eyes. "Um, I guess before I say anything, I should apologize for violating the rules and coming directly here to meet Jake before we had a chance to get to know each other through letters or phone calls. I know you specifically discourage that."

"We have found that a sort of 'blind date' meeting usually puts too much pressure on the couple. If they know a little something about each other first, their initial meeting won't be so awkward."

Catherine bit her lip. "I think I'm suddenly finding out exactly what you mean."

"I don't understand. Are you saying you now wish you hadn't come?"

"Oh, no. I'm glad I came." Catherine took a deep breath and released it slowly. "Jake's a dream." Her cheeks filled with color. "But I find that I'm suddenly in a panic. What if he doesn't like me? He didn't seem too happy to see me."

Becky touched Catherine's arm. "No, don't worry that he won't like you, Catherine. In fact, I already told him I'd ask you to leave if he wasn't comfortable having you here."

She bit her lip again. "You did? What did he say?"

Becky smiled and patted her client's arm. "He said he'd like you to stay."

Catherine's face brightened. "He did?"

Becky nodded.

Catherine's hand flew to her heart. "Oh, boy. Now I'm really nervous. That's the other thing I want to talk to you about, Becky." She fanned a hand over her face. "I'm suddenly realizing that I'm too frightened to stay on my own, but I just can't leave now that I'm here."

Becky guessed what was coming next. She bolted from the bed. She folded her arms and faced Catherine, trying not to panic.

Catherine stood and placed a gentle hand on Becky's arm. "Please, Becky, say you'll stay a few more days, just until I see how things are going to go between Jake and me. I promise I won't ask you to stay one day longer than is absolutely necessary."

Becky shook her head vigorously. "Catherine, I don't think so. You and Jake should be alone. The two of you don't need me."

"I didn't mean you should chaperone us. I meant

I'd like you to stay around for moral support. I just couldn't stand going through this all by myself. I'm afraid I'd leave and give up the one thing I've been searching for all my life." Catherine wiped away a tear rolling down her cheek. "You're my only chance for happiness, Becky. You've brought me this far, couldn't you please stay a while longer?"

Becky's heart punched her ribs. Staying and watching Jake with Catherine would be torture.

Catherine bit her lip once more. "I'd be happy to pay an increase in fee."

Coupling people was her job. It was time she started acting like the professional matchmaker she was. Becky jutted her chin forward. She had told Jake she always did everything she could to keep her clients satisfied. And she did. "Of course, if it's that important to you, I'll stay a few days until either you're comfortable with Jake or you've decided he's not for you."

Catherine released a giant sigh. She placed her hand over her heart and sat back on Becky's bed. "Oh, thank you, Becky. You've saved my life."

"It's part of my job. I've been keeping in touch with the office from here. I guess I can continue that way a while longer." She slid back into her bed as Catherine stood. "I'll tell Jake in the morning that I'm going to stay a few more days."

Catherine walked to the rollaway. "Now I can sleep well tonight," she said, slipping under the covers.

Becky turned out the light. *I wish I could,* she thought as she laced her hands behind her head. But she knew she wouldn't rest. Thoughts of Jake would plunder her mind as he had plundered her lips. She'd have to find a way to put her heart on ice while she wore the garb of a Chicago businesswoman. Catherine must never know of her personal involvement with Jake, and Jake must have no reason to think there might be a chance she'd changed her mind about leaving because of him. She had to be one hundred percent professional one hundred percent of the time.

Becky woke an hour or so after sunrise. To her amazement, Catherine was already gone. Becky yawned and stretched. Unlike her, Catherine was obviously a morning person. Perhaps it was a trait she developed growing up on a farm.

Shaking her head to wake herself further, Becky decided she'd better get up and face the day with all its confrontations. She briefly showered and dressed, then went to her laptop. She put Catherine's profile on a floppy disk, then took it to Jake's computer to print it out. He should have access to it, the sooner the better.

When Catherine's bio had printed out, Becky removed the disk and returned it to her room. Then she took a deep breath and went to find Jake.

As she reached the bottom of the stairs, Becky heard Jake's deep, sexy voice. Her heart stopped along with her legs. She willed them both to resume their momentum. She'd assumed Jake was talking with Sam, but when she nearly reached the kitchen door, she realized she was wrong.

"I know what you mean," she heard Catherine say. "We did that too."

Becky pressed her back against the wall next to the door. She knew she should either make her presence known or turn around and go back to her room. She couldn't convince herself to do either. She didn't want to hear Jake and Catherine getting along just fine, but something wouldn't allow her to move away from them.

Jake laughed heartily. "And this was outside Peoria?"

"Yes," Catherine replied. "I know Peoria isn't exactly the area people think of when they think of dairy farms, but that's where ours was."

"Did you have to get up early to milk the cows?" Becky heard Jake take a sip of coffee.

"Oh, I loved to get up early. It was the evening milkings I didn't like." Catherine sipped too.

"You had to milk cows in the morning and the evenings? Didn't one of your parents or siblings have to take a turn?"

"Actually, my brother Mickey who was a couple of years younger than me was supposed to do the evening chores, but he was about as dependable as a car without an engine."

"Sounds like you got the short end of that stick."

"I did, but life has a way of catching up with people. Because of his laziness, Mickey ended up working in a dead-end job and marrying a woman as easy to live with as a permanent case of hives." Catherine took a long sip. "I guess sloth has its price."

"So he got his just desserts, huh?"

"I don't know about that." Becky surmised from the long pause Catherine took she must have been eating something.

Then Jake said, "So what was so bad about doing the milking in the evening that wasn't so bad about doing it in the morning?"

"Well . . ." Catherine paused, and Becky imagined she was biting her lip again from the sound of her voice. "You see, I dated a lot my last two years of high school. And, well, if I had to milk the cows in the evening I'm afraid my boyfriends would often catch me before I had a chance to finish the job and take a shower. I don't have to tell you I didn't smell like a gardenia blossom after spending a couple of hours around cows."

Jake chuckled, and Becky envisioned the light in his eyes that always appeared when he was amused. "Ouch. That must have been pretty embarrassing for a teenage girl."

"Yes, but I always made a joke out of it, and the guys were pretty good about having to wait." Becky heard Catherine take another sip of coffee. "I could never make plans for the early movie, though, and then nine times out of ten, I'd fall asleep during the late one because I was so tired from getting up to milk the cows before school." She giggled. "I wasn't too much fun on a date, but boys kept asking me out anyway."

"I'm not surprised," Jake said. "You're lovely."

"Why, thank you, Jake."

Becky couldn't listen anymore. She dragged herself back to the stairway. She grasped the post at the bottom of the railing for support as her strength left her body. For the first time in fifteen years, she wished she wasn't so good at her job. It sounded as though she'd made another perfect match.

She walked up the first two stairs and sat down on one of the steps. She took Catherine's profile and read it over once more. She truly was perfect for Jake.

Becky released a huge sigh. At least one good thing would come of Jake's and Catherine's instant connection with each other. Catherine wouldn't require her to stay longer than a few days. Becky was sure of that.

"Good morning, Becky."

She snapped to her feet and nearly tumbled off the stairs. "Jake!" She pressed her hand to her heart. "I didn't hear you come up."

"You looked pretty engrossed in what you were reading."

Becky glanced at the paper, then back up at Jake as she handed him the bio. "It's Catherine's profile. I figured you'd like to have it. I didn't give it to you before because I hadn't had a response from her." Becky looked toward the kitchen as Jake took the paper. "Where is Catherine?"

Jake folded the paper and placed it in his back pocket. "She's out with Blackjack. She saw her through the window, and had to go meet her. I guess she likes dogs."

"Yes, she does."

Jake stepped closer to Becky. He draped his arms across his chest. "Are you still planning to leave today?"

As Becky shook her head, she saw Jake's lips curve upwards. "Catherine wants me to stay around for a while. She needs a little moral support."

"I see," he said, rubbing his chin.

Becky reflexively touched his forearm. "Oh, Jake, she isn't afraid of you or anything like that. She's just a little nervous out here all alone where she doesn't know anyone. You understand."

He glanced at her hand on his forearm.

Becky jerked it back. "Is it all right with you if I stay a few more days?"

Jake unfolded his arms and thrust his hands into his pockets. "Becky, I never wanted you to leave in the first place. I think you know that."

"Please, Jake, we're talking about Catherine now."

He slowly moved his head up and down as he pierced her with his eyes. "All right, if you say so."

"Do you . . ." Becky cleared her throat. "What do you think of Catherine so far?"

"So far?" Jake pulled his hands from his pockets and folded his arms once more. "So far I'd say she seems very nice. We had quite a pleasant talk over breakfast."

"Good." Becky tossed her hair over her shoulders. "Jake, I need a favor."

"Anything, Becky. You know that."

"Well," she said, trying to avoid direct contact with his scorching gaze, "I've got a new project I'd like to start working on while I'm here. I mean, it looks like I'll have some time, so I was wondering if you'd mind if I used your computer from time to time, especially when I need to print things out."

Jake lifted a nonchalant hand. "No problem. Use my office, if you'd like." He closed the space between them, touched his fingers to Becky's chin. "You know I'd be willing to share everything with you, Becky."

Jake's name rang out from the kitchen.

"I, I guess that's Catherine," Becky said, trying to speak over the lump in her throat. "I'd better go upstairs and get to work." She spun around and scampered up the steps.

"Becky," he called after her.

She stopped and turned around. "Yes, Jake?"

"There's no need in your starving just because you want to put some space between us. Sam left you some breakfast in the kitchen."

"I almost forgot. Tell Sam I'll be down in a few

minutes." As she reached the top of the stairs, she heard Catherine join Jake at the bottom.

"There you are," she said coyly, gazing up at him. "Are you ready to give me the grand tour?"

Becky watched Jake press his hand into Catherine's back. "Ready," he said, smiling down at her. He glanced at the top of the stairs one more time, then led his new guest toward the kitchen.

Catherine wanted to see the horses first. She'd fallen in love with horses as a child and even had one of her own on her family's farm.

"Jake," she said, taking a brush and letting herself into one of the stalls as soon as they entered the barn, "I hope you don't mind. I just have to brush this one right away. It's been such a long time since I've even touched a horse."

"You weren't kidding when you expressed your fondness for horses, were you?" Her enthusiasm delighted him. She was like a child who had begged for a bike for years and finally got his wish.

Catherine shook her blond locks. "I could do this all day," she said, taking nice long strokes over the animal's hide. She petted him and stroked his mane. "What's his name, Jake?"

"Farewell." As he said the name the familiar pain tugged inside him.

Catherine scowled and glanced toward him. "Farewell? That's rather unusual."

Jake leaned against the rails of the stall Catherine occupied with the horse. "It was a gift from my dad. He bought it for me shortly before he died. I didn't know until afterwards."

She went to him, placing her hand on the arm he'd draped across the top of the rail. "I'm sorry, Jake.

Then he's a special horse, isn't he? Is he your favorite?"

He shook off the hurtful feelings always evoked by thoughts of his father. He brightened his voice and grinned. "I don't have a favorite."

Catherine drifted her gaze from stall to stall. "You have some magnificent animals. If I were you, I couldn't choose a favorite either." She went back to brushing Farewell.

Jake watched her stroking the animal with expert ability, then glanced toward Scout, the horse he usually rode, the one he'd ridden with Becky in his arms, the one she'd watched him put away after their day with Jimmy. She hadn't even left yet, and he missed her more than he could stand. How would he ever survive after she was gone?

Suddenly feeling locked into something he couldn't escape, Jake turned and walked to the door of the barn.

"Jake, where are you going?" Catherine shouted to him.

He smiled at her and replied, "I'll be back in a few minutes."

He pounded the ground toward the back door of the house. He had to see Becky. He had to make her understand how he felt. If necessary, he'd force her to admit how she felt about him.

When he reached the steps to the back door, his feet died in their tracks. He found himself completely immobile. He'd held her in his arms in that very spot. He'd kissed her until her limbs had gone limp, and she'd weakened him just as severely.

Suddenly Jake bent and picked up a rock. He threw it as hard as he could toward a huge tree in the middle of the yard. By heaven, he and Becky belonged together, and he wasn't going to wait another minute to tell her.

"You hunting birds with rocks, Jake?"

He snapped around to find Lucas Rolland mounted on his horse leading a string of three stallions. "Lucas. I forgot you were bringing the horses by today."

"As long as you don't forget to pay for them," the blond cowboy said as he dismounted. "Want to look them over before you take delivery?"

"Why? You wouldn't cheat me, would you?"

Lucas grinned broadly and playfully shoved Jake's shoulder. "Maybe with a woman, buddy, but not on a business deal."

Luke's reminder of the fact that he'd spent time with Becky nearly drove Jake wild. Before he threw his fist into his friend's face, Jake forced himself toward his new string of stallions. "Want to help me get them into the barn?"

Lucas tied his mount to the hitching post near the back door of the house and went with Jake to the barn. As they entered, Luke halted to an immediate stop.

"My, my, Jake," he said, staring at Catherine, "none of your hired hands ever looked this good before."

Jake walked to the stall and took Catherine's hand as she exited it. He brought her to Lucas. "This is Catherine Worthington. Catherine, this nasty varmint is Lucas Rolland."

Luke's eyes drank in Catherine's shapely figure, so well-defined in her blue knit shirt and jeans. He shook her hand. "I certainly hope you're going to stay for a nice long visit."

Jake could have sworn he saw Catherine blush as she said, "I think I just might." She didn't take her eyes off his charming friend as she continued to hold his hand.

Jake looked from Catherine to Lucas. "If the two of you don't mind, we've got some horses to put away." Then to Lucas he said, "Thanks, Luke. I'll get a check to you in a couple of days." Jake took the horses.

Lucas looked at Jake as he dropped Catherine's hand. "Sounds good, Jake." He tipped his hat to the lady. "Nice to meet you Miss Catherine." He abruptly turned and left.

In a matter of seconds Catherine was at Jake's side helping him to put away the horses. She knew exactly how to handle them. As Jake watched her tuck the last animal into its stall, he was touched with the way she seemed to fit right into his life. It was as though she was born to be on a ranch, maybe his ranch. He wondered for a moment if perhaps the computer did make more sense than the heart when it came to picking mates for life. He decided in that instant that he owed it to himself, maybe even to Becky, and certainly to Catherine, to get to know the computer's choice for him. He wanted a wife, and maybe a computer match truly was a better one than one he could make for himself.

Chapter Nine

The next few days brought Jake closer to Catherine. They spent all of their time together, and Jake found himself growing very fond of her. She fit his life perfectly. Everything about being on his ranch was second nature to her. But she wasn't Becky.

When he lay awake in his bed at night, it wasn't thoughts of Catherine that robbed him of his sleep. Becky stole his rest, disrupted his breathing, looted his heart, swindled him out of common sense and embezzled his love. She wounded him and filled him with ecstasy simultaneously. He wished he'd never met her, yet he died at the thought of never having known her. He ached for the mercy of her departure, but, if she left, she'd take his breath, his heart, his soul.

When Jake forced reason to plan his life, he saw Becky as a barricade between him and Catherine. If there were no Becky, he'd propose to Catherine immediately. Becky had done her job flawlessly. She'd found him a woman he could spend his life with, a companion, a wife beautiful enough to enjoy in every

110

way. But Catherine would never bring him the rapture he knew from one glance of Becky's dark eyes or a toss of her hair. She'd never consume him as Becky did with a gentle touch of her fingertips. Yet, he was convinced Catherine could offer him contentment, children, and a satisfying life. He hadn't asked for more. He hadn't expected anything beyond compatibility.

Becky had been taking her meals in her room most of the time, leaving Jake and Catherine alone. On the morning Jake had decided that perhaps it was time to move on with his life without Becky, she happened to join Catherine and him for breakfast.

Sam served the three of them in the dining room. "You eat hearty now," he said, placing plates before each of them. He turned and walked as far as the doorway before he cranked his head back, eyeing Catherine. "Ms. Worthington," he said, rubbing his chin, "I was a wondering, would you maybe like to go into town with me to get supplies for my kitchen? You was tellin' me about some recipe you liked for fried chicken. I thought you might help me pick up what I need to make it and help me with that this afternoon."

Catherine sat up straight in her chair. "Sam, I'd love to, but I was going with Jake to check out one of the herds." She looked at Jake and tilted her head. "What do you think, Jake? Would it be all right if I went with Sam? I'd love to have the chance to make my special fried chicken for you."

"Whatever you want to do is fine with me, Catherine." Jake sipped his coffee as he glanced toward his housekeeper. "I think we can trust Sam to take good care of you."

"All right then, Sam," Catherine said, smiling at the older man, "in that case I'd love to go with you."

Sam nodded vigorously. "It'll be my pleasure." He covered his face with a smile bright enough to light a city. "And Miss Montoya can go with Mr. Jake to the pasture. She likes that sort of thing too, done it a couple of times before."

Catherine's head snapped toward Becky. "Really, Becky? You enjoy checking on cattle? You've done it before?"

"Not until I came here," Becky said, a touch of anxiety in her voice, "but I really did enjoy having Jake show me around. I think the ranch is fascinating."

"It's settled then," Sam said, a smug look of satisfaction sweeping across his face. "I'll take Ms. Catherine into town while Mr. Jake takes Miss Becky out to check on the herd. All right, Mr. Jake?"

Jake squirmed and stretched his long legs under the table. "Whatever the ladies want to do is fine with me." He kept his exterior cool, but the steak he'd put into his stomach shoved a hoof into his ribs. He couldn't believe he was taking Becky back to the pasture by the river. Then suddenly he realized Sam had given him the perfect opportunity to learn with finality whether he was ready to move on with Catherine or if he still had a chance with Becky. Today would bring him the path to his future, and he'd know by sundown whether it would be with Becky or Catherine.

Jake had planned to drive Becky to the pasture in his truck, but she'd told him she preferred to ride horses. She surprised and delighted him with her request. Traveling over the trail they'd taken in the buggy last time, side-by-side on horseback, Jake felt completely comfortable with Becky. He could tell she enjoyed riding this time much more than she had the first time, and she looked as much a part of her environment as the wildflowers did. For the first time she appeared relaxed and natural with him. He surmised that the reason might be that this time she wasn't working. She wasn't examining him for her files. She was merely on an outing on a beautiful day with a man she'd come to know rather well. Jake wondered if he'd see a new side of Becky, and he anxiously looked forward to finding out.

"We'll check on the herd right away, unless you need to rest a while first," Jake said as he and Becky approached the pasture.

"No, I'm fine. I'm much more comfortable than the first time we did this." Becky shifted in her saddle. She shaded her eyes. "I see a few of the Herefords over there," she said, pointing.

"Let's go," Jake said, gently spurring his mount. His lips curved upwards slowly hearing Becky's words. She referred to the herd by their breed name instead of just calling them cows or cattle. There was a little bit of rancher in her already.

Within a few minutes the two of them were riding with the herd. As Jake scanned his cattle for any problems, he heard Becky call out.

"Jake, look!"

He rode to her and looked in the direction she was pointing. He dismounted and went to help her off her horse. Together they went to the newborn calf Becky had spied.

"He's so sweet," Becky said tenderly as she dropped to her knees and snuggled her cheek into the top of the tiny heifer's head. "And look how he can walk already."

Jake chuckled at another display of her lack of ranch savvy. "I'm afraid he's a she, and they walk right after they're born."

She fluffed her hand over the calf's curly reddish-brown hide. "How wonderful. I didn't know that."

Jake bent next to her. "Let me show you something else they do. Give me your hand."

Becky entrusted her fingers to the cowboy. He gently put them up to the calf's mouth. The baby took them and suckled on them.

Becky yanked her hand from the heifer's mouth. "Oh, my. What's she doing?"

Another chuckle rumbled Jake's ribs. "She won't hurt you," he said, taking Becky's fingers and placing them near the calf's mouth again. "Go ahead."

Becky gave her hand to the baby cow, and the little heifer pulled at it enthusiastically. Becky laughed. "It feels funny, but nice, like when a cat rubs on your legs or a dog licks your chin."

"Something like that." Jake helped Becky to her feet. "Watch where you walk, Becky. A lot of cattle have been through here."

Becky looked around. "I'll be careful."

He led her back to the horses and helped her into the saddle. "We'll finish checking the herd, then we'll eat."

"I hope Sam packed us something good. The ride has given me quite an appetite." Becky patted her stomach.

"You're not afraid of gaining weight anymore?" Jake asked, teasing.

"Not since I lost four pounds the last time we spent

a few days getting out to see your cattle. Jake, maybe you should call your ranch a spa and start charging people to come out and work for you. I think they'd be real happy with all the weight they'd lose working in a saddle while they ate their fill of steak and ham and fried potatoes."

Jake tipped his hat back slightly and grinned. "Maybe I should."

When the cattle had been surveyed and passed the inspection, Jake took Becky to the same spot under the ancient oak where they'd eaten with Jimmy. He laid the blanket, unloaded the lunch from the back of the saddle, and staked out the horses. He'd watered the animals on their way from the herd to their picnic spot. Blackjack hadn't followed them this time, so the two of them were completely alone.

"What would you like to do first, go fishing or have our meal?" Jake asked as he walked back from where he'd secured the horses. He held up the fishing gear. "I brought this along since I know how you enjoy fishing."

"Ooh, I don't care how hungry I am, I do like to fish more than just about anything." Becky jumped up from where she had seated herself and took some of the gear from Jake. "You didn't fish with Jimmy and me the last time we were here. You do like to fish, don't you Jake?"

"Sure," he said, taking her arm with his free hand as they walked toward the river. "I just didn't want to intrude on you and Jimmy. It was more fun watching you."

"I bet," Becky said, slipping a disbelieving smile over her face.

"Do you, Becky?"

"Do I? Do I what?"

"Bet?"

"You mean gamble?"

"Yeah, gamble."

Becky lifted a shoulder. "Rarely, but I've done it."

"So you're not averse to taking a chance on something, then, huh?"

Becky stopped and turned to face Jake. "What's all this about?"

Jake shrugged. "I was wondering if maybe you'd like to place a wager on who lands the biggest catch of the day."

"That sounds interesting," Becky said, licking her lips in anticipation of winning Jake's little challenge.

"Are you picking up the gauntlet?"

Becky eyed him as though he were a pigeon. "I'd shake on it, but my hands are full."

"That's no problem." Jake bent towards her and kissed her. "The bargain is sealed."

Surprise filled Becky's dark eyes. "Sealed," she repeated. She took several steps, then turned back to Jake. "But we haven't said what we were betting."

"Yes," Jake said reflectively, "Something must be at stake." He studied Becky's expression. He knew what he'd like to win from her, but what would she like to win from him? "I say," Jake said hesitantly, "if I win, you have to be completely honest with me about whatever I ask you."

"That doesn't sound like much of a bet," Becky said, squinting against the sun. "Whether you win or not, you could ask me anything, and I'd give you an honest answer."

Jake doubted that. "Then it'd be a bet you wouldn't mind losing."

"All right, Jake, if that's what you want. I'll ask the same of you because there are a few things I'd like to know that you wouldn't tell me before." She nodded carefully. "It's a bet."

He kissed her again.

She smiled up at him.

"Just to seal the bargain," he said defensively.

The fish weren't biting. Jake and Becky tried every trick they knew, but neither of them secured so much as a nibble.

At last Becky felt a tug on her line. "It's about time. I was about to give in to my rumbling stomach and quit." She wound her reel and began to pull in her line. "Jake, I might need some help with this. It's heavy."

Jake dropped his rod and instantly went to help. He put his arms around her as he helped her pull in her catch. "We might lose it, Becky. It's pretty heavy. The line might break."

"Easy, Jake, easy." Becky carefully wound the line as Jake secured the fiberglass rod. "What?" Becky lifted her brows as she caught the first glimpse of her quarry. "What is it, Jake?"

The cowboy stepped back from her and went to the shore. He pulled what Becky had snagged from the water and held it up for her to see.

"It looks like a wheel."

"That's exactly what it is, from an old bike." Jake pulled the garbage to the shore.

Becky put down her rod and plopped onto the bank. "That's enough. I'm ready to give up if you are."

"As long as you don't make me build a fire to roast that tire for our dinner, I'm ready to quit too."

"You're sure?"

Jake nodded. He picked up the gear and pulled Becky to her feet. "Let's go see what Sam packed us before we starve."

"Sounds wonderful," Becky said, taking some of the equipment from Jake. "You can pay up after we've eaten."

Jake halted and spun toward her. "Pay up? Becky, we didn't get any fish."

"True, but our bet concerned who made the biggest catch of the day, not who caught the biggest fish. Not only did I make the biggest catch of the day, I made the only catch of the day." Becky resumed her walk toward the ancient oak. "A bet has to have a winner, and, no matter how you look at it, I won this one."

Jake chuckled and joined her in several long strides. "If you say so." He liked this new side of Becky. She definitely seemed to be more relaxed. It reminded him of the first night she spent on his ranch when they went out to look at the sky. She'd been as playful as a child, the way she was right now.

When they'd eaten their fill, Becky gathered their things and returned them to the pack. Jake secured it to Scout's saddle.

Becky stretched out in the shade. Jake sat beside her when he returned from the horses. "What a beautiful day, Jake. I've never known another time more peaceful or more full of contentment. You know, being here has changed everything for me."

"It's changed everything for me too." He locked his eyes on her.

Becky turned to her side and let her fingers toy with a tear in the blanket. "I guess it has, hasn't it?"

Jake nodded as he removed his hat and placed it at

the edge of the wool beneath them. He intensified his gaze and pointed it directly into her dark eyes.

She looked from the broken threads her fingers touched up to Jake. "Are you ready to pay up?"

He softened his eyes. "I guess so." He lifted a curious brow as he wondered if she wanted to know from him what he needed to know from her.

Becky didn't wait long to satisfy his curiosity. "I want to know about that painting over the fireplace," she said flatly. "Why have you kept the identity of the artist such a secret?"

She'd stupefied him. He'd been so sure she'd wanted to talk about them, their feelings for each other. "Well." He struggled to get his thoughts together. "It's no secret, really. It's just that the first time you asked me, I didn't know you very well. That's why I hesitated to answer you then." Jake stretched on his side and lay face-to-face with Becky. "The artist, Rusty, was my mother."

Becky sprang to a sitting position. "Your mother? How fascinating."

"She was very talented, but she didn't start painting until shortly before she died. She'd always wanted to, but she never found the time. Finally, she made her art a priority, but *Hidden Meadow* was the only work she ever completed."

"Hidden Meadow," Becky repeated. "What a beautiful name. But, Jake, I don't understand the meaning. Does it have anything to do with all the little creatures in the meadow scene?"

Jake placed his hand along his hip. "That's exactly what it is about. The small animals, the gopher, the snake, the mouse, the prairie dog, and all the other critters represent the small things in life. You know, our little problems. Mom painted the picture filled with the little creatures that we often don't see to show how life can become cluttered with and taken over by little things if we let it. She always said it's the little things that give us the biggest problems. But there is another way to look at the picture too."

Becky pulled her knees to her chest and widened her eyes. "What's that, Jake?"

"Mom also said it's the little things that give us the greatest joy, and one's life can be taken over by those things too."

"I think I'd have liked your mother, Jake. She sounds intriguing."

Jake nodded as he touched Becky's cheek. "You would have, and she'd have liked you too."

Becky let go of the legs held tight to her chest and returned to her side. "Do I get another question?"

"Shoot."

"My room, that is your guest room. Your mother decorated it for a special reason, didn't she?"

"It was her studio as well as a guest room."

"And she decorated it the way she painted *Hidden Meadow,* with all kinds of little things that mattered to her on the walls." Becky's voice trailed off as she observed Jake's uneasiness at discussing his mother.

Jake sat up and leaned back on his hands. "Even if I didn't win our little contest, Becky, I think you should let me ask a few questions too." A change of subject wouldn't hurt, and he had a few things he needed to know.

"Sure," Becky said, waving a nonchalant hand. "Ask away."

Jake narrowed his eyes and bore them into Becky's.

"What did you mean when you said being here has changed everything for you?"

Becky stretched out on her back and raised her eyes to the tree above them. "It means lots of things, Jake. In many ways, I'm a completely transformed person. Everything that's happened since I came has put me on a new path, made me see my life with different vision." She turned back to her side. "I'm ready to put away old things and try new."

Jake's heart skyrocketed. She was talking about him, her, them. He lay back on his side close to her. He touched her cheek with his fingers. "I knew something was different about you, Becky. You've made an important decision about your future, haven't you."

"Yes, I have," she said, taking the strong fingers that caressed her cheek and placing a kiss on them. "And I have you to thank for it."

Jake squeezed her hand. "You don't have to thank me, Becky."

"Whether I do or not, I'm grateful to you just the same. And I guess I'm grateful to your mother too. Her painting must have had a subliminal effect on me. Or maybe it's the solitude and peace of the ranch that leads a person to reflect on what's really important to her."

She was confusing him, and he didn't like it one bit. "Becky, I'm not sure I know what you mean."

"We're both at a crossroads in our lives, Jake. Only I didn't know about my turning point until I came here and met you. You have known for some time that you were ready to move your life in a different direction. Now I know that too."

Jake took her hand and toyed with her fingers. "Becky, just what changes are ready to make?"

She took a deep breath and blurted out her news. "I'm selling my business."

Jake could hardly believe his ears. "You're selling *Match Made in Heaven?*"

"Yes."

"Are you sure you really want to do that?" Jake squeezed her fingers in his.

"I am." She stared directly into his eyes. "I guess I discovered what your mom did. You shouldn't put off something you really want to do until it's too late."

He squeezed her fingers again. "And what is it you really want to do? Move to the country?" he asked, hoping with every cell of his body.

"I'm planning to move, all right, but not to the country. I'm going to New York. I'm going to write books."

Jake dropped her hand and leaned back on his elbows. "New York? To write?"

"Yes," Becky said, sitting up. "I've always wanted to write. I'd like to write romance stories and self-help books about relationships and finding the right partner." She suddenly cut off her words and gave him a peculiar look. "Is anything wrong, Jake?"

He sprang toward her, took her hands and pulled her against him. "I thought when you said you were selling your business you were finally ready to admit how you feel about me, about us. I thought perhaps you'd finally come to your senses and decided you want to take a chance on us."

"Jake," Becky said catching her breath, "I don't know what to say."

He grasped her jaw firmly. "Don't say anything, Becky." He lowered his lips to hers and devoured her, ingesting her a little at a time. His appetite piqued, he released her jaw and gathered her close, crushing her to his chest. He felt her weaken in his arms and meld to his body. He increased the intensity of his ardor, and Becky responded with an eagerness that exposed her complete vulnerability to his seduction. Jake lured her to the brink of irrepressible desire, then abruptly released her. She sat back on her heels, breathless and trembling.

Jake took Becky's hand and pulled her to her feet. Her unsteadiness was victory to him. She could move to New York and write all the books she wanted, but she would never forget him. He'd seen to that.

He lifted the blanket and shook it in the wind. "We'd better get back to the ranch," he said flatly.

He tied the blanket roll to the back of his saddle and brought the horses to where Becky was standing on shaky legs. He lifted her onto her mount, then boosted himself onto Scout's back.

As they rode side by side in silence, Jake glanced at Becky from the corner of his eye. He sighed and wiped a hand across his jaw. He hadn't realized until that instant she was astride Farewell.

Chapter Ten

Jake hadn't said a word on their ride back to the ranch. He'd created a tomb of silence that nearly drove Becky mad. She wanted desperately to dig her way out of the smothering void, but her mind was as helpless as she had been tucked inside Jake's embrace. She had no idea what to say to him to get him to talk to her again.

She'd broken her leg as a child. The broken bone had been the worst pain she'd ever experienced—until the ride back to the ranch that day. She had told Jake that coming to the ranch had changed her life. It had in so many ways, but what her arrival in Montana had done more than anything else was confused every cell of her body.

She'd thrown the rulebook out the window that first day at Jake's. Before she even knew who he was, she found herself in his arms enjoying every second his warmth touched her so intimately. After she learned his identity, she didn't care that he was a client. She let herself get close to him, touch him, kiss him, even fall in love with him. She couldn't forgive herself for her breech of ethics. Her guilt consumed her so completely that she'd decided to sell her business. She'd crossed a line, and there was no turning back.

Ironically, freeing herself from her business was the one thing that would allow her to stay with Jake as she was sure he wanted. Yet, she couldn't find the strength to forgive her transgression, or the courage to risk a relationship that might end in the tragic way her parents' marriage had ended.

Jake didn't see that she'd done anything wrong, and he was willing to risk everything to take a chance on her, on them. If only she could see through his eyes. Maybe then she'd have the grit to confess her maddening love for him.

Becky walked to the window, sat on the seat, and looked out into the yard. She saw a piece of Jake in every building, and she saw his family and years of tradition in the trees that had stood long enough to have witnessed the many lives of all the people who had ever occupied the land.

Everyone who had tried to tame the wild acreage into a home took tremendous risks. It didn't always pay off, but sometimes the rewards surpassed expectations.

Jake had taken huge risks. He'd left home to earn his way through college. He'd secured work on Wall Street, which must have seemed as foreign to a country boy as anything could be. He'd earned the fortune he'd set his sites on, then came back to Montana to tackle a new challenge. Now, in the middle of his life, he stood ready to take another huge gamble, one that could cost him a broken heart or give him greater joy than he'd ever imagine.

Becky glanced toward the barn. She saw Jake go inside. She raised her hand to her heart. "I love you, Jake," she whispered.

She tilted her head back against the molding of the window. Suddenly it came to her. She hadn't lived her life without risk. Didn't she mortgage everything she owned to start her business fifteen years ago? Hadn't she put herself through college? Wasn't she among the first of the computer dating services to guarantee satisfaction in a business where guarantees are impossible? She'd risked so much, but she'd won more than she'd ever lost.

And didn't she win just today?

Becky ran to the door. She threw it open, scampering down the hall and stairs. She barely acknowledged Sam as she passed through the kitchen. She had to see Jake—right now. She had to tell him that she loved him, that she was willing to take a chance. Dear heaven, how she loved him.

She slammed the back door and jumped down the stairs. She covered the distance from the house to the stable in record time. She stopped just outside the door. She leaned against the siding and summoned all her strength.

Jake's deep voice broke into Becky's gathering courage. "So what did you do when your little sister gave mustard to your pet rabbit?"

"I put molasses in her chocolate milk," Catherine said smugly.

Their banter and laughter froze Becky in her tracks.

"Jake, Scout acts as if something's wrong with his leg. Is he all right?"

"Sometimes I think that horse is too smart for his

own good. He moves like that when he wants attention. Go over there and pet him. You'll see he's fine."

The talking stopped a few moments, then resumed.

"You're right," Catherine said over a jolly giggle. "He's not moving funny anymore."

"I told you. He's a peculiar one."

"Jake, I'm really getting to like it here," Becky heard Catherine say.

"I'm glad," Jake said softly. Becky knew the tone he used with her, and she imagined the softness in his eyes that accompanied it. "You fit on a ranch like you were born to it."

"Well, I was raised on a farm. There isn't much difference, you know."

Becky regained her mobility. She stepped away from the wall that had magnetized her. She aimed herself toward the house. She couldn't talk to Jake now, but she would talk to him later. She had to before things went any further with Catherine.

An hour before the evening meal, Catherine came to the guest room in search of Becky. "May I bother you for a moment?"

Becky looked up from her laptop. "Sure. What is it?"

"I wanted to invite you to join us for supper tonight," Catherine said, her eyes glowing. "I'm making the fried chicken Sam mentioned at breakfast this morning. Can you join us or are you too busy?"

Becky stretched and yawned. "I'd be happy to eat with you."

"Fine. We'll see you in an hour."

Catherine left, and Becky wished she could take back her acceptance. It wouldn't be easy to break bread with a woman she was about to wrong. Yet, she'd made up her mind. She'd tell Jake how she felt about him, and let the chips fall where they may. Whatever the consequences, she had to take the risk.

Becky finished some on-line business, then cleaned up for supper.

Sam and Jake were in the kitchen when Becky came in. She went directly to Jake and whispered, "I need to talk to you later. Is that all right?"

"No problem," Jake said.

Catherine came to the kitchen and took Jake's hand. "Let's go into the dining room. Everything's ready."

To Becky's relief, the meal was a pleasant one. The conversation was dominated by Catherine's outgoing personality and stories of her trip to town with Sam. Becky breathed a sigh of relief that Catherine hadn't asked about her ride with Jake. She'd never have been able to hide the guilt she'd have felt about betraying Catherine then, or for the betrayal that was about to come.

When the meal was over, Catherine called Sam into the dining room. She told him to sit down next to Becky. She took a china cup from the buffet and poured Sam a cup of coffee. Then she returned to her seat next to Jake and wrapped her hands around the cowboy's arm.

Catherine looked from Becky to Sam to Jake with glistening eyes. She glanced back at Sam and Becky. "Jake and I have something to tell you." She looked up at Jake.

He pulled his arm from her hands and draped it around her shoulders. He smiled at her. Looking into her eyes, he said, "I asked this lovely young lady to marry me . . ." He looked to Becky. "And she said 'yes.' "

Becky's heart plummeted. She looked at Sam, and saw disapproval fill his eyes. She turned back to Catherine and forced words from her mouth. "Congratulations," she said, over the obstruction in her throat. "I don't know what to say."

Jake pinned his eyes to her. "Don't say anything, Becky," he said slowly.

He'd said those words to her earlier that day. As she remembered, she died inside.

Becky stood at the same time Sam did. "I've got some work to do up in my room."

"And I've got dishes that need tending in the kitchen," Sam said. He thrust his hand toward his boss. "Congratulations, Mr. Jake. I hope you know what you're doing." He nodded toward Catherine. "Best wishes Ms. Worthington. You better be sure you want to be stuck with this polecat."

Catherine's sparkling eyes swept Jake's handsome face. "I'm sure," she said, snuggling into Jake's side.

Becky turned to leave, and Sam followed her. As she made her way to the staircase, he dogged her steps until he caught her shoulder and turned her around. "It ain't right," he said, fire in his voice. "You're the one, not her. And you'd better do something about it, Missy, or I will." He stalked to the kitchen, and, in a moment, was clanging the dishes and cookware loud enough to drown out a tornado alarm.

Minutes later Becky stared at her computer screen. She opened her word processor and chose the new document option. She wrote and centered a title. *Love's Greatest Sacrifice.* She spaced down a few lines then typed: "Chapter One. Becca hadn't intended to fall in love, but she did. Jack had promised to marry someone else, though Becca loved him with all her heart. She wouldn't stop him. He'd made his choice. If he'd have loved her a little more, waited for her a moment longer, Becca would have never let him go. But life doesn't exist on if's, and Becca couldn't change fate. She'd lost Jack, and she'd never get him back. It was time to move on."

Becky sat back in her chair and sighed. "How's that for moving on?" she murmured to herself. "It's time I start a new chapter in my own life." She returned her fingers to the keyboard, and started hammering out her first book.

Before she finished the first ten pages, the room grew dark, signaling the approach of the ten o'clock hour. Becky stretched toward the window and peered out. The sky was clear. She'd love some fresh air. She walked to the door and let herself out. She traced the steps of the hall and descended the stairs. A breath of relief escaped her when she saw the living room was empty. Without hesitation, she went to the front door and stepped outside.

The crisp air washed over her, soothing her muscles like a massage. Becky combed her fingers through her hair and then breathed in deeply. She brought her hands down and gave them a shake. Taking another deep breath, she went down the stairs along the broken-brick sidewalk past the spot where her pumps had staked her to the ground that first day. Slowly she turned and examined all she saw in the moonlight. This is the way she wanted to remember Jake's ranch, filled with moonbeams and glistening stars.

The constellations vibrated with the same intensity they'd shown her on her first night in Montana. Becky stepped slowly over the graveled driveway, flashing her eyes from her pathway to the heavens and back. Sooner than she'd expected, she found herself at the corral, staring at the horses.

She'd learned most of their names by now, except for the three new ones. Jake hadn't named them yet, and he didn't care for the names Lucas had given them. Luke named all his horses after baseball players.

Becky walked around the corral to get closer to the horses. She recognized Scout immediately. She identified Daisy, Bullet, Cactus, Sugar and—her heart leaped to her throat. She'd tried all afternoon to remember the name of the mount she rode with Jake earlier that day, and, finally, it came to her, Farewell.

She put her hands on the top rail and leaned her face into them. She was going to miss the ranch so much.

"What are you doing out here, Becky?"

The voice behind her was Jake's. The sound of it fused her to the fence. "I . . . ah, I came out to see the horses. I've grown very fond of them."

He stepped closer to her, placed his hand next to hers and leaned against it. "I see." With his free hand, he waved away a mosquito near Becky's face. "You mentioned earlier that you wanted to talk to me about something."

Becky's knees weakened. Obviously she couldn't tell him what she'd intended now that he was engaged. She had to think of another reason she might have to talk with him. "I don't suppose . . ." She looked at the horses and avoided the gaze she felt piercing through her. "I don't think Catherine needs me to stay any longer, Jake. I'll see if I can get a flight back to Chicago tomorrow."

He touched his hand to her hair. "You're welcome to stay as long as you'd like, Becky." He pulled his hand back. "But I know you're probably anxious to get back to the city and sell your business so you can move to New York and start your new life."

She picked at the wood of the rail with her finger. "Yes. Yes, I am."

As Jake touched her hair gently, Becky feared she'd come apart. "I want to thank you for everything you've done for me, Becky," Jake said softly. "I guess your computer was right."

"If you say so. Are you sure you don't want to meet the other ladies I gave you profiles for?" She had no idea how she was able to maintain her business-as-usual attitude.

A chuckle rumbled through him. "Now it's a little late for that, don't you think?"

Becky smiled, but she still didn't look at him. "I suppose it is."

"So you're leaving tomorrow . . ."

She picked at the wood again, staring at her fingers. "There's no reason for me to stay any longer."

"I guess not . . ."

Suddenly she turned to face him. "Thanks for everything, Jake."

He raised his hand to her cheek and cupped her face. "It was my pleasure." His voice dripped with sensuality.

Becky nearly fainted under the masculine power he held over her. "Oh, Jake . . ." A tear trickled from her eye. "I don't know what to say."

He touched his thumb to her lips. "Don't say anything, Becky," he whispered in his husky voice. He palmed her other cheek and held her face so gently between his hands.

Becky kissed his thumbs as he traced her lips once more.

Jake's icy eyes intensified.

Becky's knees began to melt.

He kissed her forehead.

Becky closed her eyes and kissed the fingers resting near her mouth. *One last kiss,* she wished.

"Jake!"

He didn't move.

Becky opened her eyes and found his gaze boring down on her. "Jake, it's Catherine."

Still holding her cheeks, he nodded and closed his eyes. When he opened them again, he said, "I know."

"Jake!"

He traced her lips one more time with his thumbs and drilled his gaze deeply into her eyes. "I'll never forget you, Becky." Suddenly he dropped his hands and turned away.

Catherine was much closer now. "Jake!"

"I'm here by the corral."

Catherine walked up to him and planted a kiss on his cheek. "Oh, hi, Becky. I'm glad you're here. I've got something very important to ask you."

Becky looked down and wiped her eye. She turned towards Catherine. "Sure, Catherine. Anything."

"Now I know this is a major, major imposition, but would you mind staying another two weeks? I'd love for you to be my maid of honor, and I could use all the help I can get planning the wedding."

"Oh, no, Catherine," Becky said. "I'm sorry, but that's out of the question. Besides, your sisters should help you with that."

"Becky, please," she said, placing her hands on Becky's forearms. "I don't want my family to know about my wedding until it's over. They'd drive me nuts. Everyone would have a different opinion, and we'd all end up fighting."

"I don't know," Becky said reluctantly.

Catherine turned to Jake and gripped his arm. "Jake, you talk her into staying. If it weren't for her, we wouldn't even be getting married." She turned back to Becky. "Please, Becky. Stay and see your match through to the final vows."

Becky looked from Catherine to Jake.

"We'd love to have you stay, Becky," he said, circling Catherine's waist with his arm.

She stared into Jake's eyes. No way could she watch the two of them together for two more weeks. She absolutely had to get back to Chicago and on with her life. No. No. No. "Yes, I'd love to," she said, instantly wanting to kick her agreeable little mouth.

"It's settled then," Catherine said victoriously.

"I do have one condition, though," Becky added. "Jake, I'm afraid I'm going to have to continue to impose on you for use of your office."

He nodded toward her. "Of course. Use it as much as you want."

"Thank you," Becky said. She was suddenly very nervous. She needed an escape. "I'm tired." She faked a yawn. "I'm going to turn in."

"I'll see you in a minute, Becky," Catherine called as she walked away.

When Becky was out of hearing range, Jake turned to Catherine. He furrowed his brows. "I thought you were going to ask your friend in Peoria to be your maid of honor. Why did you change your mind?"

Catherine shrugged. "I don't know. I was talking to Sam about the wedding after supper, and he suggested it. He said, 'Miss Becky should be at Mr. Jake's wedding,'" she said, imitating Sam's voice, "and I thought, maybe he's right. Then I realized that if I asked Christine to be my maid of honor, she'd never be able to keep the news of our wedding a secret. Before you'd know it, the ranch would be crawling with Worthingtons." She stretched up and kissed Jake lightly on the lips. "And I want our wedding day to be perfect."

Jake draped his arm over Catherine's shoulders and aimed her toward the house. He took the hand she offered him and entwined it with his own as he reflected on Catherine's explanation. So Sam had suggested Becky stay. Jake didn't know whether to thank him or fire him, but he definitely owed Sam something.

Chapter Eleven

Becky threw herself into her new writing projects as soon as she got up the next morning. For the next couple of days she worked on both her novel and the outline for her relationship book.

As she studied which angle she might use on the nonfiction project, Catherine came to her to ask for help.

"I've been on the Internet shopping nonstop for the last two days, Becky," Catherine said, wiping her wrist over her forehead. "I need to see the inside of a real store and touch some actual merchandise before I make my decisions about the wedding. Would you come into town with me?"

Becky stood from the window seat where she'd been working. She plopped her notes down on the calico-covered cushion. "Sure. I could use a little contact with society too." She placed her hand over Catherine's forearm. "Only don't expect to find much. The pickings are mighty slim, as Sam would say."

Catherine grinned. "I know, but it doesn't hurt to

look. And you never know, if I don't find something I'd like to buy, I might at least get an idea that will help." They moved toward the door. "And two heads are better than one. And shopping is shopping— whether it's State Street or small town Main Street."

As they motored out of Jake's driveway, Becky and Catherine decided to go to Carington. It was the largest town in the area, only twenty miles away. Since the town boasted a population of nine hundred and forty-three, it was large enough to have groceries, gas, a department store and a small medical center along its quaint, charming main street which was called States Street. When they reached Carington, they drove directly to its one small department store.

Catherine and Becky were surprised to discover that Becker's Department Store even had a tiny wedding department. Catherine was thrilled to have the chance to try on several gowns. She'd been reluctant to order one over the Internet. A wedding gown deserved to be special in every way. A woman needs to touch her wedding dress before she buys it, Catherine had told Becky.

Becky sat in the waiting area while Catherine changed from one gown into another. Even though there were only several selections to choose from, Catherine found a dress she was very pleased with.

Next they went to the linen department. Again the choice was limited, but Catherine wanted to see if she could find something new for the bedroom she and Jake would share in less than two weeks.

As the ladies browsed the inventory of sheets and comforters they were joined by Lucas Rolland.

"My, my," Lucas said, removing his Stetson, "if it isn't Miss Becky and Miss Catherine." He bowed his head toward them. "How lovely to see you." Then to Becky he said, "I thought you were leaving last week."

"I was," she said, glancing toward Catherine, then back to Luke, "but I had a change of plans."

Lucas put his hand over his heart. "Well, I'm cut to the quick that you didn't call me for a date." He turned to Catherine, took her hand and kissed it as he locked eyes with her. "If Miss Becky isn't interested in me any longer, perhaps I might have the pleasure of getting to know you a little better, Miss Catherine."

Talkative Catherine seemed to have suddenly lost her voice. "I . . . I . . . "

Becky folded her arms and slid a grin over her face. "She's trying to tell you that she's engaged."

Becky's news had no effect on the eyes Lucas riveted to Catherine's gaze.

"Lucas," Becky said, touching his forearm and shaking it slightly.

"Yes?" His eyes didn't move.

Becky nudged Catherine. "You tell him, Catherine."

"What?" she asked blinking, then glancing at Becky.

"Tell him you're engaged," Becky said, chuckling at the comical scene.

Catherine's focus returned to Luke's gaze. "I'm engaged." She pulled her hand from him. "I'm engaged to Jake Ruskin."

Lucas straightened to his full six-feet, two-inch height. He raked his fingers through his curly blond hair and lifted his broad shoulders. "Why that varmint is too old to get married to anyone, let alone a pretty young thing like you," he said to Catherine.

"Nevertheless, we are getting married." She lifted

the bag she had in her hand. "I have the dress right here."

"They're tying the knot a week from Saturday," Becky explained. "I'm going to be the maid of honor."

"And you're going to be the best man, aren't you Lucas?" Catherine glanced back at the navy blue eyes that had hardly left her.

"Me? The best man?"

"I know Jake is going to ask you." Catherine put her hand on his uncovered forearm. "You'll do it, won't you?"

He covered her hand with his and lowered his voice. "I'd be right proud to, ma'am." Then, turning to Becky, he said, "Say, I've got a fine idea. You probably noticed that Carington is having a festival this week. There'll be a big dance on Saturday night. How about the best man taking the maid of honor and the bride and groom joining us?"

Becky started to shake her head when Catherine shouted, "We'd love to. It sounds absolutely heavenly."

Becky's head switched from side to side movement to up and down. "Yes, we'd love to."

Lucas returned his hat to his head. "All right, ladies, I'll see you Saturday. Becky, I'll come by for you at seven, and Catherine, I'll see you and Jake at the dance."

Catherine bowed her head forward and blinked her eyes. "Yes, and I'll have Jake call you to make your best man status official."

Lucas tipped his hat and disappeared out the front door.

Catherine placed her hand over her heart and sucked in air as though she'd been drowning. "Becky! He's gorgeous, and what a charmer. You should have a great time Saturday night."

"Yeah, great," she said with about as much enthusiasm as she'd have if she were attending her own funeral. The last thing she needed to see was Catherine in Jake's arms all evening, but she couldn't get out of the date now.

Saturday night came quicker than Becky had anticipated. Keeping busy with her writing projects had filled in the bulk of her time. In addition, she'd contacted a broker to sell *Match Made in Heaven*. He'd told her he had several prospects who were looking for something new and different to invest in, and encouraged her that with her record of success, he'd have an easy time finding a buyer.

Catherine was still trying to decide what to wear when Becky descended the stairs in the new sundress she'd bought for the casual affair. It had been very warm all week, so the bright yellow and white halter dress seemed to be the perfect choice.

Jake rose as Becky neared the last two steps. He went directly to the staircase and stretched out his hand. His eyes slowly traced each of Becky's feminine curves before they returned to her gaze.

Becky took Jake's outstretched hand and went down the last two steps. "Good evening, Jake."

He smiled broadly. "You're breathtaking." He kissed the fingers he held so gently in his hand.

Her throat tightened. "Thank you." She removed her hand and let her eyes inspect him as he'd examined her. "I don't think I've ever seen you in twill pants and a knit shirt. Cute little alligator," she said, touching him above his breast pocket. "I like the look on you, but it doesn't seem right. To me you're a blue jeans kind of guy."

Jake rubbed his hand over his chest. "To me too. I haven't worn anything like this since I moved from New York. I'm not crazy about teal and khaki, but Catherine picked it out, and I didn't want to disappoint her."

Becky leaned back on her heels and rubbed her chin. "Now I could see Lucas in those type of clothes. In fact, I have, but you, Jake . . ." She shook her head.

Standing at the foot of the stairs, Becky and Jake chatted until Catherine appeared wearing a simple black dress with a V neck and black sandals. "Is this okay?"

"You look very nice," Jake told her.

"It's perfect," Becky said, offering a more reassuring feminine opinion.

Jake suggested he and Catherine wait with Becky until Lucas arrived, but she told them to go on without her and her date. She convinced them that Lucas would come for her soon.

Before her escort got there, Becky found Sam and told him she may get a business call from Bob Kline. She instructed him to take a careful message and tell Mr. Kline she'd return his call first thing in the morning.

Lucas arrived a few minutes late wearing navy twill pants and a gray and navy striped knit shirt. He gave an ample apology for his tardiness and sufficient admiration for Becky's appearance. Then he led her to his black Cougar and took her to the dance.

The country-western band began playing at eight, and Lucas was quick to lead Becky to the dance floor for a whirl over the polished hardwood of the old-time dance pavilion. He held her close and moved her with the agility of an expert. A few dances later, he led her to the refreshments and bought her a soda. He took one for himself, then invited her outside.

Lucas led Becky to an empty bench and asked her to sit. He sat next to her, soda in one hand and the other draped over her neck, his fingers gently massaging her nape. "Jake told me all about the two of you," he said softly.

Becky's gut wrenched. All about them? "What do you mean?" She hoped her voice didn't reveal the anxiety in her mid-section.

"About you being a matchmaker and finding him Catherine."

"Oh, that," she said, relieved he hadn't meant something more personal.

"Yes, that. What else?"

Becky sipped her soda. She lifted a shoulder. "I don't know. It's just that an open-ended comment like 'Jake told you all about us' is rather ambiguous."

"Yeah, I guess so."

Becky looked up at Lucas. She slid a grin over her face and cocked her head. "Are you hinting you'd like me to find someone for you next?"

Lucas kissed her lightly. "First tell me if you'll marry me," he said, grinning.

Becky kissed him and grinned back. "No."

"That's what I thought."

"So do you want me to find someone for you?"

"Not unless you can find me someone just like Catherine."

"I might be able to, but I'm selling my business. I'm through making matches for other people."

Lucas wrinkled his forehead. "Seriously?"

Becky nodded.

"Why? Didn't you enjoy it?" Lucas raised an eyebrow. "Or are you looking for a match for yourself?"

Becky quickly looked away and bolted to her feet. "Let's go back inside," she said, tugging at Luke's hand. "The music is playing again."

Jake hadn't seen Becky for quite a while. He'd combed the pavilion visually as he and Catherine danced, but he couldn't find Becky anywhere. He didn't see Lucas either. Around the tenth dance number, he finally saw Becky come in from outside, her arm laced around Luke's. His gut turned to iron. His engagement to Catherine hadn't made any difference. He still couldn't stand to see Becky with another man, and, best man or not, he wanted to take Lucas apart as much now as he ever had. Maybe more. He viciously eyed the man as Lucas and Becky approached them on the dance floor.

"What do you say we change partners?" Lucas asked as Jake and Catherine separated.

Jake forced himself to keep from grabbing Becky at Luke's welcome suggestion.

Luke smiled sardonically and said, "Becky, you take Catherine, and I'll take Jake."

The women laughed and pretended to partner up while Jake threatened to pound Lucas into the floor.

"You don't like that idea?" Lucas asked Jake in his most sarcastic tone. "Well, Catherine isn't as tall as you are, Jake, but she is prettier than a mountain stream to a parched man." He took Catherine's hand. "Would you mind, Miss Catherine?"

Catherine nodded toward him. "I'd love to, Luke."

Lucas wasted no time sweeping her into his arms and whisking her from Jake.

"Would you like to dance, Becky?" Jake asked, offering her his hand.

Becky hesitated, then pressed her palm to his. "I guess it'd be all right."

Jake pulled her close and mentally thanked the band for slowing the pace of the music to something soft and romantic. He pressed his cheek into Becky's hair and inhaled her sweet fragrance deeply. Apples and lemons. Cinnamon and vanilla. Peach, lilac. He couldn't identify one sweet fragrance from another, but Jake knew he didn't need to know its name to enjoy its sweetness. He'd memorize it and carry it with him always.

He nuzzled his cheek deeper into her hair and held her tighter. Too low for Becky to hear, he whispered into her dark locks, "This is where you belong, sunshine."

Jake lost count of the number of dances he and Becky shared. One had flowed into the next. He was totally unaware of anything but the warmth Becky burned through his body.

"Jake?" Becky said when the music stopped.

"Yes?" His deep voice was even huskier than usual.

Becky glanced around the room. "I haven't seen Catherine or Lucas for some time. Have you?"

"I guess not. They must have stepped outside for some fresh air. It is getting a little warm in here."

"Should we go look for them?"

Jake took her hand and led her back to their table. "They'll turn up sooner or later." He held a chair for her. "I'm going to get us something to drink. Would you like to have a bite to eat too?"

Becky shook her head. "Just water, please."

Shortly after Jake returned with the refreshments, including drinks for Catherine and Lucas, the disappearing couple returned.

"Where did you go?" Jake asked as he held Catherine's chair.

She scooted in close to the table. "Lucas told me there was a cougar outside. I'd never seen a mountain lion of any kind, but I knew they lived in Montana, so I wanted to see it."

Jake laughed. "So you fell for that one, huh?"

"You know what he meant, Becky?" Catherine asked innocently.

She giggled and sighed. "I'm afraid I do. Remember? I drove over with him. It is a nice car, though, isn't it?"

Catherine gave the blond cowboy next to her a playful slap on the arm. "You'd better not try to pull a trick like that on me again, big fella."

"Tricks are part of Luke's charm," Jake said, leaning forward enough to place his elbows on the table. He folded his arms and leaned into them, grinning. "It's a good thing you're engaged to me, or who knows what he might have tried once he had you alone in the parking lot."

Catherine blushed and raised her drink to her lips. She sipped nervously. "Yes, who knows."

A man in black western wear with a shimmering ten-gallon hat went to the microphone on the bandstand. "If there's a Jake Ruskin here, you got a call at the reception area. Jake Ruskin."

Eyes turned to their table, and Jake stood. "I'll be right back."

He was gone only a few minutes while he took the

call. When he returned he stared down at Becky. "It's Sam. He said you got a call from a Mr. Kline, and you need to call him back right away. It's urgent. He also said that he'd gone out to look at the horses and Sugar looked like she was going to foal early."

Becky stood immediately. "Kline is my broker. He's selling my business for me. Can I make a call from here?"

"Sure," Jake said. He pointed to the reception area. "There's a phone right over there."

Becky suddenly clenched her fist. "Shoot, I don't have Kline's number. I left it by my computer."

Jake put his hands on the back of Catherine's chair and tugged it away from the table. "You could ride home with us, Becky, and make the call from the ranch."

Lucas stood and raised his hand. "Now, hold it a minute. There's no point in ruining everyone's evening." He thrust his hands into his pockets. "Just because you two have to leave doesn't mean that Catherine and I need to call it a night too. Jake, why don't you take Becky home so you can check on the mare, and she can make her call. Catherine can stay with me, and I'll bring her home later."

Jake glanced from Lucas to Catherine. "Do you want to stay with this broken-down excuse for a country playboy?"

Catherine smiled up at Lucas. She looked back at Jake and lifted a brow. "Would you mind terribly if I did, Jake? I do love to dance, and we won't stay more than another half an hour or so. I promise."

"Whatever you want is fine with me," Jake said, scooting her chair back to the table. He raised his eyes to Lucas. "As long as this big guy behaves himself."

Luke raised his right hand. "Now, Jake, have you ever known me to be anything less than a perfect gentleman?"

Jake eyed him carefully. "Yes." He glanced toward Catherine. "Keep a close watch on him," he warned. He bent to kiss her cheek. "I'll see you in a little while."

The ride in Jake's truck back to the ranch drifted between nervous silence and small talk about each of their businesses. Yet, even though the atmosphere of the ride dripped with uneasiness, Jake hadn't wanted it to end. Any excuse to be with Becky was a good one. He'd barely wished for more time with her, when a pang of guilt hit him. In one week he was going to marry Catherine. He owed her his loyalty.

Jake helped Becky out of the truck when they reached his driveway and slid his hand to her lower back as they walked to the front door.

They'd barely stepped inside when Sam appeared. "Glad to see you two got right home," he said, seeming to squelch a grin that wanted to cover his face. "I left your message on the desk over there, Missy," he said, pointing, "and you know where the horses are, Mr. Jake." He touched a finger to his forehead and waved it toward the two of them. "G'night." He rushed to his room as though the tax man were chasing him.

Becky and Jake turned towards each other. Both of them furrowed their brows and asked in unison, "What's that all about?"

Becky laughed at the coincidence, then, calming her voice, she said, "I'd better make my phone call, and you'd better check on your mare." Becky touched Jake's hand. "Jake, I hope Sugar is all right."

He touched the tip of her nose. "Don't worry. I'm sure she's fine." He glanced down at his clothes. "I'd better change out of these foreign duds before I go outside. Blackjack won't recognize me, and I'd frighten the horses."

Becky watched him bound up the stairs. She kicked off her sandals and picked them up by the straps. Then she went to the desk to retrieve her message. The slip of paper said, "Mr. Kline, 312-555-5024, call back." She stepped to the staircase and went up to her room. As she talked on the phone with Kline she heard Jake go downstairs. Peeking out the window, she saw him enter the barn.

"Excuse me, Bob, what did you say?"

"I said you didn't have to call me back tonight. I told the person I talked to there that you could call me in the morning. There's nothing more I can do tonight anyway."

Becky plopped into the window seat. "Well, now that we've discussed things, I won't have to call you in the morning. If you want to fax me the offer, I'll sign it tomorrow." She gave Kline Jake's fax number, then hung up the phone.

Becky shook her head as she stripped out of her clothes. She decided Sam was getting confused in his senior years. He must have misunderstood Bob's message.

When Becky finished her brief shower, she peered out the window. The light was still on in the barn. The way was clear for her to go down to the kitchen for a midnight snack before Jake came back.

She scanned the refrigerator. Not seeing anything too tempting, she glanced at the corner counter. Jackpot! Sam had baked one of his world-famous cherry pies. Becky quickly heated a cup of water in the microwave and dunked a tea bag in it. She cut a piece of pie and put it on a plate. Plate and cup in her hands, she turned to go up to her room to enjoy her midnight snack.

The back door opened. "Becky," Jake said, surprised to see her in her robe and bare feet.

Becky spun around. "Jake. Is Sugar all right?"

Jake placed his Stetson on the hat rack. "There isn't a thing in the world wrong with her. She's no more ready to foal than Scout is."

Becky laughed. "Well, I think she is probably a little more ready than your stallion."

Jake went to the sink and washed his hands. "How did your phone call with Kline go?"

"Fine, but I think Sam must be a little confused. Bob said he specifically told him that I should call tomorrow morning because there was nothing he could do tonight."

Jake leaned against the sink and lay his head back for a brief moment. "I think I see what's going on here."

"Going on?" Becky stepped near Jake and placed her cup and plate on the counter. "What are you talking about?"

"Sam has let me know in his not-so-subtle way that he doesn't approve of my marriage to Catherine."

"Really?"

"Yes. He has some crazy notion that I should marry you, not her." Jake touched her cheek softly.

Becky pulled away from him. "That's ridiculous." She picked up her cup and plate. "Sam and his matchmaking. How did you ever stay single so long with a live-in Dolly Levi?" She shook her head and walked to the kitchen door on her way back upstairs.

"Becky?" Jake folded his arms and leaned against the counter again.

She spun back to face him. "Yes, Jake?"

"I've known Sam ever since I was a small boy. In all those years, he's never once tried to fix me up with anyone."

A knot tightened in her stomach. She stared a long moment at the handsome cowboy. Suddenly she dropped her gaze. "Good night, Jake." She spun back to the door and left him.

Chapter Twelve

Becky went to the window seat with her pie and tea. She set the tea on the ledge while she bit the cherry pastry and leaned her head back against the window frame. The words Jake uttered echoed through her mind. *"He's never once tried to fix me up with anyone."* She'd have bet her life Sam had made a practice of interfering in Jake's love life. She truly had been surprised that Jake had called her for help after she met Sam. Being on the receiving end of his matchmaking had convinced her that Sam must have tried to put Jake together with every woman who came anywhere near the ranch.

Things weren't at all as she'd surmised—at least not things that concerned Sam.

When it came to Jake, though, everything was exactly as she'd suspected . . . no, feared . . . actually, hoped. He hadn't left any doubt when he held her in his arms as he swept her over the dance floor. He might be engaged to Catherine, but his heart still belonged to Becky.

She sighed and set the pie down. She took the comfort cup of tea and sipped. As the warm liquid assuaged the emptiness that filled her whenever she was away from Jake's side, her mind filled with fanciful thoughts. If only a life with him were possible.

Each day she spent on the ranch brought Becky a greater fondness for its rustic splendor and beauty. She often wondered if the natural wonder she lived within was the reason she'd been able to accomplish so much in her writing pursuits. While being on Jake's ranch had caused her pain and emptiness, it had also allowed her to experience love and great inspiration. She wondered if she'd find the same inspiration among the skyscrapers of New York City.

Becky sipped again and smiled broadly. "There's always Central Park," she whispered. If it's a rural setting she needed to be inspired, surely Manhattan's bit of country would adequately supply her needs. Hadn't an afternoon in Grant Park pacified her when the clamor and congestion of Chicago's loop took its toll on her serenity?

But Central Park wasn't Jake's ranch. And none of the men in the Big Apple would be Jake.

The door opened abruptly. "Becky! You're still up."

A pang of guilt hit her as she turned to Catherine. She bolted to her feet. "Yes." She held up her cup. "Just having some tea."

"Oh," Catherine said, nodding absentmindedly. She turned away and went into the bathroom.

Becky could hardly believe what she'd just seen. It was completely out of character for Catherine to ignore her. Usually the woman talked her ear off over everything from the state of the cattle on the ranch, to the function of the pancreas, to the formation of volcanoes. Practically everything interested her, and she always wanted to talk. On a night when she'd just met all kinds of new people and danced to her heart's content, Becky thought if she was still awake when Catherine came home, she'd end up chatting with her until dawn.

She yawned and drank a little more tea. Hearing the water filling the bathtub, Becky decided she'd go straight to bed. Catherine would be in the bathroom for a good long soak. She obviously wasn't expecting a long conversation with her matchmaker.

Lying in the cool sheets, trying to fall asleep, Becky couldn't help but feel something was wrong. Catherine didn't seem like the same person she'd seen every day since the young match for Jake had arrived at the ranch. Not only was she quieter than usual, there was a completely different look about her.

Becky turned to her side. Strange, very strange.

Becky amazed herself at how much she accomplished over the next couple of days. Catherine had been keeping busy on her own and hadn't asked Becky to accompany her on any more shopping trips.

Being tired of working cooped up in her room or Jake's office, Becky charged up the battery of her laptop computer so she could take it outdoors to work. She went to the barn to ask Jake's permission to take one of the horses for a ride to the river. She thought the quiet rustling of the leaves and easy rambling of the river would evoke the right mood she needed to write her next chapter of *Love's Greatest Sacrifice*. Jake wasn't in the barn, but his foreman was. He readied Cactus, the horse she'd ridden her first day with Jake. After she packed her computer and the bag of food and drink she brought from the kitchen, Becky mounted the animal and pointed herself toward the meadow by the river.

It seemed strange covering the open territory she'd traveled before only with Jake, or with Jake and Jimmy. She was proud of this new independence and basked in the satisfaction of feeling confident enough to ride away from the ranch on her own. If anyone had told her a month ago she'd be riding a horse at all by now, she'd have told them they were delusional. Yet, she was not only riding, she was doing it without anyone else's help.

Becky smiled when she caught sight of the river. Next to the little shack in the other direction, the river was her favorite spot. She sauntered Cactus through the growth of wild flowers and guided him to the big oak tree where she'd pleasantly whiled away her time with Jake.

She dismounted and unpacked the horse. Then she led him to the river for a drink. When Cactus had his fill, she staked him out to graze. Settling the blanket on the ground, Becky sat leaning into the giant trunk of the oak tree and booted up the computer. Within minutes she began to write, the words coming as profusely as she'd hoped they would in this inspirational environment.

"Becca wanted to be alone. She'd seen Jack earlier that day, and she feared he'd seen her love for him in her eyes. Though she wanted him more than anything in the world, she'd never let herself come between another man and his woman.

"It was a beautiful day, and Jack's plantation boasted a huge acreage. Surely she could find a

small corner of it where no one would discover her.

"Though she'd worked for Jack for several years, she'd spent most of her time in the kitchen cooking meals for him and the men who helped maintain the plantation. She knew very little of the hills and hollows of Covington Manor.

"Strolling through an orchard, past a restful shady stand of maple trees, Becca discovered a nook with an old carved bench tucked into a grove of a dozen blue spruce trees. The cool air inside drove away the heat of the trail she'd walked from the house.

"Becca sat on the bench and thought about leaving the plantation. She'd inquired about a housekeeping job in Independence, and she laughed at the irony. If she secured the position, she'd be moving to the town that owned the name of the last thing she wanted. Yet, it would be even more painful to stay near what she wanted most— Jack. Seeing him at the breakfast table every morning as she served him and his new wife their meal, the two of them having spent another night of passion together, would be an unbearable affliction.

"Becca had no choice. She had to leave Jack Covington, and she had to leave him now, before he married.

"Tears tottered from her eyes, and Becca buried her face in her hands. 'I love you, Jack,' she whispered through her sobs.

"As she began to tremble in anguish, she suddenly felt a strong hand cover her shoulder. She flinched and sprang her gaze upwards. 'Jack!'

" *'Becca.'   He hunched down beside her.
'What's wrong?'*

" *'Jack, I didn't hear you come up. What are
you doing here?'*

" *'I'm looking for you,' he said, wiping her
tears with his fingers.*

" *'You are?' The trembling she'd felt a moment ago struck her again with a force greater
than any she'd ever known. Jack was looking for
her. He wanted to see her. She tried with all her
strength to steady her voice. 'What did you
want?'*

"*Jack slid next to her on the bench and took
her hand. 'I've come to ask you something very
important . . . Becca, I . . .'*"

A deep, stern voice suddenly broke Becky's concentration. "I said, what are you doing on my land
with my horse?"

Becky peered around the tree into the direction of
the angry words. It was Jake. She put down her computer and stood. "I hope you don't mind, Jake. Your
foreman was sure it would be all right for me to take
Cactus out."

The cowboy whipped off his hat and slammed his
hands to his knees. "Oh, Becky, I had no idea it was
you sitting there. I thought someone had stolen my
horse and then had the audacity to languish about on
my land." He straightened up and walked to her.

"I came out here to write. It's such a pretty place.
I figured it would inspire me." She nervously explained her actions as though she owed it to him. Then
she mentally drew a parallel between Jack finding
Becca alone on his land and Jake finding her. As color

flooded her cheeks knowing what was about to happen between Jack and Becca, Becky looked away from Jake.

"Did it work?"

"What?" she said, still looking away.

Jake lifted her chin and forced her eyes up to meet his. "Did you get inspired?"

Becky glanced at the laptop lying on the ground. "Ah, yes. I did." She turned her eyes back up to him.

He folded his arms. "Good. I'm glad." He looked around the meadow slowly, then back at Becky. "I've come out here a couple times to think myself." He walked away a few steps in the direction of Cactus. He waved his arm toward the horse. "I have to admit I am surprised to see you comfortable enough to take a horse out on your own."

"Me too," Becky said, chuckling. "But I really enjoyed it."

He walked back to her. He twirled his hat in his hands. "I just came out to check on the herd."

"By yourself?"

Jake grinned as he wrinkled his brows. "Sure by myself. Why not?"

"I mean, Catherine. Hasn't she been doing everything with you?"

Jake looked down at his hat, then placed it on his head. "Not since last week. I guess with the wedding drawing near, she's got lots to do."

"Yes, I suppose she does. I haven't seen much of her either." Becky glanced down at the laptop again. "Well. . . ."

Understanding what she meant, Jake said, "Yeah, me too. I'd better check out that herd." He stared into Becky's eyes a long moment, touched her cheek, then dropped his hand and adjusted his hat. "If I'd known I'd run into you out here, I'd have brought the fishing gear."

Becky smiled and made no effort to resist the urge to reach toward him and place her hand on his arm. "Bye, Jake. I'll see you at the ranch later."

He dropped his eyes to her hand resting against his arm and nodded. "See you, Becky."

She watched him walk away and wished he were Jack, for in the scene she was writing, Jack was coming to tell Becca he wanted her and only her. He'd called off his wedding.

Even though she was many thousands of words away from completing the novel, she couldn't wait to write the last scene. If her reality wouldn't have a happy ending, her unreality should.

Sam was in the kitchen when Becky returned to the house. "Can I fix you something to eat, Miss Montoya?"

Becky set her computer pack on the table while she tossed the remnants of her lunch into the garbage and sink. "No thanks, Sam. I'm going upstairs to work."

Sam took the dirty dishes out of Becky's hands. "Come on now, ma'am, you've been working too much. You even took your computer along when you went for a ride. I don't know how you could work on such a beautiful day." He shuffled her to a chair. "Now you sit down and let Sam get you something to eat or drink. Coffee, lemonade, iced tea, soda, cake, brownies, you name it."

Becky smirked. If he was going to be difficult, she could too. "How about a cappuccino and a raspberry scone?"

Sam whirled around and opened a lower cabinet. He pulled out a cappuccino machine. "Coffee'll be ready in just a minute." He plugged in the device and added the necessary ingredients.

Round one goes to Sam, Becky decided. She'd win round two. The old guy probably never heard of scones.

The cappuccino appliance all set, Sam turned to Becky. "The scones present a bit of a problem."

Becky folded her arms and tried to limit the size of her sarcastic grin. "Oh?"

Sam pulled a plate from an upper cabinet. "I made these this morning, but Mr. Jake prefers strawberry scones to raspberry. Will they be okay?"

Becky sobered her visage faster than a man caught cheating on his wife. "Strawberry? Yes, fine. I like strawberry scones too."

Sam served Becky her snack. He poured himself a cup of black coffee and sat across from her at the table. "Excuse me for being so personal with you, Miss Becky, but I need to talk to you."

Becky sipped her cappuccino. Whatever Sam had done to it, he'd concocted the best brew she'd ever tasted. "Talk to me, Sam?" she asked, dabbing white fluff from her lip with a napkin.

"Yes, ma'am. About you and Mr. Jake."

"What about Jake and me?" She tasted the scone and mentally shook her head. *How does that old codger know how to make these things as exquisitely as a New York pastry chef?*

"Mr. Jake told me all about why you came here in the first place. He explained that you came here to find him a wife, and you found him Miss Catherine."

"That's right." Becky sipped her coffee.

"Well, I don't like it. It's outrageous picking out a man's wife with a machine." He shoved the bag holding Becky's notebook computer. "A man can't find a woman to love with no computer. It goes against everything in nature."

Becky covered his hand with hers. "Sam, you're wrong. I've matched hundreds of couples who have been very happy and compatible together. I've used computers to pair them, and I've been very successful for fifteen years."

Sam took a long drink of black brew. "So you think you know all about men and women and putting them together, do you?"

"No one knows everything about that, but I guess you could consider me an expert in the field. Yes." Becky sat back and eyed Sam carefully. "Sam, are you trying to ask me in a subtle way to find someone for you?"

"Tarnation, no!" He pushed himself from the table and bolted to his feet. "I'm trying to tell you that you made a mistake matchin' Mr. Jake with Miss Catherine."

Becky reached for Sam's hand and pulled him back to his chair. "Sam, I think you're wrong. Catherine's a wonderful woman. She's very attracted to Jake, and she loves the ranch."

Sam folded his arms. "She might love the ranch, but she don't love Mr. Jake. And he don't love her. He loves you."

The cappuccino suddenly kicked her under the ribs. "He what?" she asked, her brows flying north.

"Mr. Jake loves you, and I'm awful darn sure that you love him. Don't you?" Sam leaned forward and bore into her with his stare.

Becky started to get up, but Sam reached for her hand and prevented her from rising. "You're not going anywhere yet, Missy. I've still got a few things I need to say and you need to hear."

She felt as though she were in the principal's office getting the scolding of her life.

"First of all, I don't care one bit who that megabitten computer of yours says Mr. Jake should marry. If it picks anybody but you, it's wrong. That machine don't see Mr. Jake's eyes when he lays them on you. I never seen joy like that in anyone in my life. You, I don't know as well, but you got something special in your look when you see him too." He paused and examined her carefully. "Miss Becky, that kind of feeling don't ever come around for most people, so when you are lucky enough to have it come to you, you have to grab on to it and not let go. No one needs a machine to tell them that."

Becky summoned all the professionalism she possessed to rebut Sam's thoroughly sensible points. "Sam, I assure you that Jake and I have no future together. He *is* going to marry Catherine in just a few days. They are perfectly suited to each other. Even if they don't love each other now, they will some day. Love grows out of friendship, and people become friends because they have common interests. I've told you before, Sam, Jake and I don't have anything in common. We're two entirely different people."

"Missy," Sam said, interrupting. "Where did you just come from before you came into my kitchen?"

"I was out on the ranch."

"Where did you go, and how did you get there?" Sam sat back in his chair, his arms tucked into his chest.

"I took a horse out to the meadow by the river," Becky replied without seeing the significance of his question.

"So you went on a horse, you, a city woman from a different world than Mr. Jake's, went all by yourself out to a pasture where Mr. Jake keeps one of his herds, right?"

"Yes, that's right. So?"

"Suddenly, those two different people don't sound so all-fired different anymore, do they?" he stated with a touch of pomposity in his voice.

Becky shook her head helplessly. "Let me see if I can make you understand."

"You give it another try, Missy."

Becky sat forward. She touched the index finger of one hand with the index finger of the other. "Jake hired me to *find* him a wife, not to *be* his wife." She touched her next finger. "I learned all I could about Jake in a few days, then searched my database for women with similar interests and backgrounds and plans for the future. I provided profiles of Jake to three women, and I gave the bios of the three women to Jake. Out of those three suitable women, Jake chose Catherine. She's a lovely, intelligent woman, and I'm sure she'll be a wonderful wife."

"You think so?"

"I'm certain of it."

Sam shifted in his chair. "Well, now, Missy, I got to agree with you on one thing. I do believe that Miss Catherine will be a good wife."

Becky's face brightened. She'd finally gotten through to the old man. She stood as Sam did.

He walked to the sink and placed their empty cups inside. He turned back to Becky, folded his arms and leaned against the counter. "Yes, I think Miss Catherine will make a right good wife indeed, but not for Mr. Jake."

All of her frustration returned. "Sam, you still don't understand."

"There's some confusion here, all right."

Becky animated her hands as she talked. "Sam, lasting relationships are based on compatibility, a sharing of interests. Once we feed the profiles of people into a computer, it can predict very accurately who is suited for whom. It's almost never wrong. I know. I've seen it succeed for fifteen years."

"I hear what you say, Miss Montoya, and I believe you are very good at your job. Maybe you're right about Miss Catherine and Mr. Jake. Maybe they'd make a right compatible match."

"Finally," Becky said sighing her relief.

"But he ain't ever gonna look at her the way he looks at you." He stood erect and shoved his hands into his pockets. "That computer may know thousands of other people, but it don't know Mr. Jake. I do. And I know Mr. Jake wants you, and I sure as heaven think you want him too."

Becky turned to leave.

"And I think you know it too, Miss Becky," he called as she left the kitchen.

Chapter Thirteen

Jake threw the bale from the hayrack onto the stack near the barn. He was grateful to have the physical job of moving hay bales. The intense manual labor helped him use the energy from bound-up nerves to do something constructive. He'd been using most of his high-strung attitude against his help in a very negative way. When his foreman suggested he take his nasty temper to the field and use it productively, Jake realized he probably had a point. The bales needed to be moved, and Jake needed to release his constrained nervous energy.

After two days of pitching the cumbersome livestock food, Jake's temper hadn't quelled. He slammed everything he touched.

On the Thursday before the wedding, Jake was in the kitchen crashing dishes and banging doors as he looked for something to snack on.

"What's all the noise about?" Sam asked, scolding Jake as though he were a child.

Jake looked up from his perch next to one of the

lower cabinets. "Where are the dad-blasted corn chips?"

"We're out of the dad-blasted corn chips," Sam replied sarcastically.

Jake stood and lengthened his extensive stance. "I'm a wealthy man, Sam. I should never be out of corn chips." He tugged at the waistline of his jeans. "Do I have to make them myself out of my own corn?"

Sam stretched up to his own fullest height, falling short of Jake's by several inches. "I've had just about enough of your edginess, Mr. Jake. I ain't gonna take it one more minute." Sam reached for Jake's arm and shoved him toward the table. "Now you sit down over there, and I'm gonna get some food into you. Maybe you're cross because you haven't been eating your meals lately. So I'm gonna stuff you with food."

"You don't need to treat me like a child," Jake said, stubbornly standing next to his chair.

"Don't I? I ain't seen you behave like this since you was eleven years old and had to give your first speech in front of the class. You was as nervous as a mouse cornered by a tomcat. If you're going to act like a child, I'm going treat you like one." Sam stomped his foot. "Mr. Jake, you sit down."

To his own amazement, Jake smiled. He pulled out his chair and seated himself, stretching his long legs under the table. "What're you going to make me to eat?"

"Leftovers that you didn't eat the last three days. Steak, beef stew, hamburgers and potatoes—fried, baked and mashed. And you'll eat every bit of it. Then you'll be too full to be ornery."

Jake watched in amusement as Sam skillfully operated the microwave oven. As soon as he'd heated an entree, he'd hand it to Jake and tell him to dig in. Hungry as he was, the cowboy couldn't eat as fast as the older man could reheat so several plates of beef and potatoes rested on the table when Sam finished his job and joined Jake.

"Help yourself to some of the grub, Sam."

"No, thanks. You're eatin' just fine. You can handle it all. I've got me some talking to do, and you got to do yourself some listening." Sam leaned forward in his chair and narrowed his focus on Jake. "You still going through with this wedding on Saturday?"

Jake swallowed. "That's right."

Sam shook his head vigorously. "You ain't suppose to do it, Mr. Jake. If it was the right thing for you, you wouldn't be so cranky. Maybe we could all stand you again if you called it off."

"This is none of your business, Sam," Jake said firmly.

"Baloney, Mr. Jake. I've known you nearly all of your life, cared for you, been right fond of you. Now I ain't gonna say you made a mistake asking that Miss Montoya here to find you a wife. A man needs a wife. He ain't whole until he has a good woman to share himself with. Bringing Miss Montoya here shows that you know that too." Sam shifted in his chair. "But that matchmaker's computer is all wrong, Mr. Jake. Miss Catherine isn't the one for you." Sam raised his hand in front of him. "Don't get me wrong. Miss Catherine is a fine woman. She's right nice and real friendly, but she don't make you happy, Mr. Jake. She makes you ornery like you been all week, and you get meaner each day the wedding gets closer."

"Sam," Jake said, patting the older man's arm, "I'm

sorry I've been so unbearable these past few days, but it isn't Catherine's fault. In fact, outside of breakfast, I've hardly seen her this week." Jake stretched to see into the living room. "Is she here now?"

"No, she ain't. She's been gone since right after breakfast, but that ain't the point, Mr. Jake. The point is she don't make you happy. Don't you want to be happy, Mr. Jake?"

Jake finished the stew and thought as he chewed. He swallowed and sat back in his chair. "Happy?" He lifted a brow. "I never really thought about it. I'm not taking a wife to be happy. I'm getting married because I want children. I need an heir."

"Don't you care if you're happy?" Sam looked at him with lines on his face sharp enough to cut rock.

"I told you, I never thought about it. I guess I'm happy enough as long as I have my ranch."

Sam shook his head. "No, sir, Mr. Jake. Your ranch ain't near enough. You're a good man, the best I ever seen. You deserve a woman that makes you so happy you don't even remember you have a ranch." Sam softened his voice. He reached for Jake's forearm and touched it gently. "That woman is upstairs right now, Mr. Jake. She's the one for you. There ain't no mystery to it. Your eyes give away your lost heart each time you look at Miss Becky. That's why I ain't saying bringing her here was a mistake. Miss Becky is the one for you, Mr. Jake, and you know it."

Jake dabbed at his mouth with a napkin. He pushed himself away from the table. Standing and walking towards the door, he stopped and turned back to his housekeeper. "Sam, did it ever occur to you that you don't know everything?"

"Yes, sir, Mr. Jake, but not this time," he said, grinning.

Jake nodded toward him and turned away. He walked up the stairs and into his office. "Oh, excuse me, Becky," he said, seeing her sitting at his computer.

"I'm almost finished, Jake. I'm doing a little printing." She turned her chair toward him. "Actually, I've been doing a lot of printing this week. I ordered a bunch of office supplies to replace what I've used."

"Thanks, but it wasn't necessary."

Becky bent toward the printer. "There. All finished." She rose from the chair. "It's all yours."

"Thanks." She brushed by him on her way out of the room, touching her body to his. He couldn't help but recall what Sam had said about Becky being the one for him. If he thought he'd have a chance with Becky, he'd marry her in a heartbeat. She'd make him happier than he'd ever thought possible. She already had. But he knew she'd never be interested in marriage. She'd made that clear too many painful times already.

Jake sat in his chair and spun it around to face the computer screen. Becky hadn't closed out her file. He couldn't resist the urge to read what she'd been working on:

Becca watched him from her bedroom window. She knelt next to the window and rested her chin on the sill.

She'd seen him lifting, toting and pitching many times on his plantation, but she'd never seen him work with such ferociousness as he did that day. Something must have upset Jack to make him work so hard. He moved as though he were hurting deep inside.

She wanted to ease his pain. More than anything she longed to hold him in her arms and comfort him, but that would never happen. He'd get his comfort from the woman who'd stolen him from her, and she'd get no comfort from anyone.

Jack glanced toward the house, and Becca jerked from the window. What would he think if he saw her spying on him? He might fire her, and then she'd be without a job. Even worse, she'd have to leave him sooner than she'd planned. That she could never stand. She loved him too much.

Jake leaned back in his chair and whispered, "Pretty intense."

"Jake?"

He spun around. "Yes?"

"I left my disk in your computer." She walked to the desk and bent over it, leaning into his personal space. "Do you mind?"

He waved a hand, giving her the go-ahead to finish her task. He inhaled deeply as she moved so close to him. All the memories he'd made holding her at the dance a few days ago flooded back to him, and he almost grabbed her and pulled her onto his lap right there. He could hardly resist the urge to feel her in his arms again. He yearned to taste her sweet lips. His precious Becky, lost to him forever.

Becky clicked the mouse and closed the file, then ejected the disk from the drive. "Thanks."

"I hope you don't mind. I couldn't resist the temptation to read a little of what you wrote."

Becky snapped to attention. "You did?" Her cheeks turned red. "What did you think?"

"I think you have a lot of talent, and you'll probably do as well in your next profession as you did in your last."

"I hope so." She held up the disk. "Got what I came for. I'd better get back to work."

"Becky?"

She stopped just outside the door. "Yes?"

Why had he called her back? "Ah, good luck."

"Thanks."

The cowboy spun back to his computer. He clicked and brought up the files he needed to work on. His concentration waned as thoughts of Becky penetrated his mind the way her lingering scent perforated his air. He typed, clicked, cursed his mistakes, and made corrections. He had work that needed to be finished before his wedding.

Jake threw his head back and crushed his hands to his face. He ordered himself to forget all about Becky and Catherine and Sam and his wedding, commanding his mind to complete the task at hand. Two hours later, the twenty-minute job was finished.

Saturday morning Jake rose even earlier than usual to take care of the chores he needed to complete before his march down the aisle.

Although he hadn't told Catherine, he'd purchased tickets for them to go to Bermuda for their honeymoon. He had decided they needed to start their life together right by being completely alone in a beautiful, romantic place. Catherine had never been to an island, and she'd told him she'd always wanted to visit a nice, warm one.

As Jake pitched hay into the feed bunks of the cattle in the yard, he thought about the day and what was to come. In a few hours he'd be exchanging vows with Catherine. He'd promise to share his life with her. The thought of getting married suddenly didn't frighten him as it had all week. Having a wife and a family was going to be a wonderful new experience for him. The thought of a little boy or girl calling him "daddy" delighted him. He smiled as he stabbed another bundle of alfalfa and threw it over the fence into the cattle trough. He was going to be a daddy.

Doubts about Catherine sneaked into his happy thoughts of parenthood. He'd seen so little of her this past week. He wished he hadn't been so preoccupied with his own wedding jitters to seek out Catherine and make sure she was all right. He chastised himself for being a neglectful husband even before he was married. He vowed he'd never be remiss in his husbandly concern again. He'd make a conscious effort to give his wife everything she deserved, especially himself and his time. He could delegate more chores to his hired help, and that's just what he'd do.

Jake came into the house at nine to shower and dress for his noon wedding. It was to be a small affair with only a few friends and his workers. He'd ordered a catered dinner to take place after the exchange of vows. Catherine had attended to the details of the menu, the flowers, and decorations for the hall they'd rented for the dinner. With all the time she spent away from the ranch this week, Jake felt sure the old church hall would be completely transformed into something very special under Catherine's direction. He looked forward to seeing the results of her efforts.

As was his habit after he showered, Jake went to

the sink to shave. He pulled his kit from the cabinet and plopped it on the counter. When the leather pouch hit the Formica, a piece of paper fell from it.

Jake frowned and picked up the paper. He opened it and began to read:

Jake,

We're sorry to do this to you, buddy, and we hope you can forgive us both. We just couldn't help ourselves. We've fallen in love. By the time you read this, we'll be married and flying to Hawaii. We only hope that someday you can find someone who makes you as happy as we are. We'll come by when we get back from the islands.
Catherine and Lucas

Jake wiped the steam from the mirror and stared at his face. He couldn't believe it. He wasn't getting married after all. He wasn't going to have children. Catherine had run off with his best friend. Her children would belong to Luke.

He put the letter down and lathered his face. He shaved because he didn't know what else to do. The note had shocked him, stung him to the core. After all he'd been through, he wasn't getting his wife or his children, and he never would. He couldn't go through any of this again.

When he'd dressed in jeans and a blue work shirt, Jake went downstairs.

"Why ain't you dressed for the wedding?" Sam asked, twisting his face.

"There isn't going to be a wedding," Jake replied hastily as he poured himself a cup of coffee.

Sam's face shone like a spotlight. "Hallelujah! You finally seen the error of your ways!"

Jake sipped his hot liquid and smiled crookedly. "I didn't, but she did."

"What do you mean? She don't want to get married?"

"Not exactly." Jake sipped again.

"Boy, sit down. You don't make no sense. Are you and Miss Catherine getting married or not?"

Jake leaned against the counter. "I'm not, she is." He drank again from his cup. "She ran off with Lucas Rolland. They're on their way to Hawaii right now."

Sam stood next to Jake. He rested his hand on his boss' shoulder. "She done the right thing, Mr. Jake. If she had feelings for Mr. Luke, she had no right to marry you. Both of you would have regretted it."

Jake straightened up. "Sam, as long as my plans for the day have been changed, I'm going out to take a look at the acreage that Jenkins wants to sell. Pack me a lunch. I'm taking Scout."

"Sure thing, Mr. Jake, but don't you think you should tell Miss Montoya that the wedding is off? It might make a difference to her," Sam said subtly.

Jake finished his coffee. "Of course it'll make a difference to her. She was going to be the maid of honor, and she's the one who brought Catherine and me together. It'll make a big difference to her." Jake reached for his hat.

"That ain't what I meant, Mr. Jake."

"Sam," Jake said, turning from the hat rack to his housekeeper. "I'm going out to get Scout. You have my lunch packed in five minutes, or you're fired. Got that?"

"Five minutes. Yes, sir, Mr. Jake," Sam said as he

started to pull food from the refrigerator. "Your lunch will be ready. Maybe when you get back from that Jenkins land you'll be ready to talk to Miss Becky the way you really should."

Jake turned a clenched jaw on Sam and narrowed his icy eyes in the older man's direction. Then he reached for the door and let himself out.

When Becky finally woke she jumped from the bed as though it were on fire. How had she slept until ten? She glanced at the rollaway bed. Where was Catherine? She grabbed her robe, slid into it and cinched it tightly around her waist. She bolted from her bedroom and flew to the kitchen.

"Sam, what happened? Why did you let me sleep so late? Where is everyone?"

Sam stepped from the sink to Becky and took her hand. "Calm down. Miss Montoya. There ain't gonna be a wedding today."

"They postponed it?"

"No, Miss Catherine decided she'd rather marry Mr. Lucas Rolland instead of Mr. Jake." Sam squeezed her hand, then let it go.

"Lucas? She's with Lucas?" Deep wrinkles lined her forehead.

"That's right. Guess she don't put no stock into computer matchups either." Sam folded his arms and eyed Becky carefully.

Becky gave him a sarcastic smile. "I guess not." She looked around the kitchen. "Well, if there isn't going to be a wedding, I guess I'll go ahead with my plans and leave a little earlier for the airport." She tucked her hair behind her ears. "Sam, I'd appreciate it if you'd fix me a tray of breakfast and bring it up to my room." She left the kitchen before he could respond.

Putting her things together didn't take long. It wasn't even noon by the time Becky had packed, showered, and tied up some loose ends on her writing projects. Sam had told her when he brought her breakfast that Jake had gone off to look at some land. She'd intended to tell him good-bye, but, now that she'd lost her chance, she felt relief settle over her. It wouldn't have been an easy thing to do, bidding Jake farewell. Maybe he wasn't looking forward to an exchange of good-byes any more than she was. That would explain his leaving. Of course, being jilted was reason enough for a man to want to be alone.

Becky hauled her belongings to the living room and piled them by the front door. Then she went out to take a final tour of the ranch. She walked first to the corral. Only a few horses were inside. Most of them were at work with the ranch hands. She leaned against the fence and watched the remaining animals graze in the mid-day sun. She moved on to the cattle lot, the garden, and the shelter belt. Blackjack caught up to her by the toolshed.

Becky scrunched down next to the frolicking dog. "I'm going to miss you, Blackjack." She took another look around the perfect layout of Jake's ranch. "I'm going to miss everything and everyone so much." Tears fell on her cheeks, and Blackjack whined as though she understood that she'd never see Becky again. Becky fluffed her hand through the dog's thick black fur once more, then stood and returned to the house, wiping the tears from her face.

She was grateful Sam wasn't in the kitchen as she

went to the sink to wash her hands. She peered out the window, and more tears ran down her cheeks.

"Looks like you're ready to go, Miss Montoya," she heard Sam say from behind her.

She kept her eyes focused on the view out the window. "Yes, I'm ready."

Sam came up to her and put his hand on her shoulder. "You don't have to go, you know."

Becky wouldn't look at him. "You know I do, Sam."

The older man touched her chin and turned her to face him. When he saw her tears, he jerked his hand away. "Why, Miss Becky, you're crying."

Becky wiped her hands over her face and forced a smile. "Sam, that's one of the things women do, didn't you know that?"

"I guess so," he said nervously. "Miss Becky? Are you sure I can't talk you into staying at least until Mr. Jake comes back?"

"No, Sam, but you can help me with my luggage."

"I'll take it right out to the car." He seemed happy to have something to do that would take him away from a crying woman.

"And, Sam, make sure my boots are in the car. I wouldn't want to forget them." She definitely didn't want to leave the gift Jake had ordered for her the first day she arrived.

In a matter of minutes, Becky was on her way back to Chicago with all the things she'd brought to Montana and a few more, including a generous lunch Sam insisted on packing her.

More tears trailed her cheeks as she turned out of Jake's driveway and onto the gravel road that led away from him. "Good-bye, Jake," she whispered. "I'll never forget you."

Chapter Fourteen

Jake returned to the ranch after he assessed the value of the Jenkins land and decided he'd make an offer. He went into the house through the back door. As he washed his hands at the kitchen sink, he looked out the window and begin to mentally write the letter he planned to compose with his offer for the Jenkins land.

Suddenly, he noticed the space where Becky usually parked her car was empty. His heart sank. She was gone. He'd never see her again.

He turned off the water and reached for a towel. As he dried his hands he wished he could wash Becky from his mind and his heart as easily.

"Mr. Jake, you're back," Sam said, coming into the kitchen. "You don't have a moment to lose."

Jake straightened up. "What's wrong, Sam? Did someone get hurt?"

Sam put his hands up in front of him. "No, no, everyone's fine. But Miss Becky, she left more than an hour ago. You've got to hurry to catch up with her.

Mr. Jake, you got to go get her and bring her back here. This is where she belongs."

Jake threw the towel onto the counter. "Sam, you've got to stop pestering me about Becky. I tell you, she left because she doesn't want to stay here. Believe me, if I had thought for one moment I had a chance with her, I never would have proposed to Catherine in the first place. Becky has made plans for another life, plans that don't include me."

"Mr. Jake, I think you're wrong. I think if you were to talk to her, you'd find out that she loves you, and she loves your ranch." Sam put his hand on Jake's shoulder. "She was crying before she left, Mr. Jake. It nearly broke my heart."

Jake looked at Sam thoughtfully. "She was crying?"

Sam nodded. "I think it was because she didn't want to leave."

Jake took a deep breath. He leaned his backside against the counter and folded his arms. He thought for a moment, then shook his head. He wasn't going to let himself be drawn back into believing he might have a future with Becky only to learn once more that she didn't want him. It took him long enough to get her rejection through his thick head the first time.

He stood up straight and pointed himself toward the door. "I'm going up to my office to work."

Sam grabbed his arm and yanked him to a halt. "No, you ain't. Before you go anywhere, I'm gonna tell you that you have to go after Miss Becky, and I'm gonna tell you why."

"Don't you think you've told me before? I don't see how repeating yourself is going to make a difference, Sam."

"Please, Mr. Jake, sit down and humor an old man,"

Sam said, using the tone that always made Jake give in to whatever his friend wanted.

"All right, Sam," Jake said, seating himself at the table. "Go ahead. You tell me why you know better than I do what's best for me."

Sam sat across from his boss. "Mr. Jake, you remember my Mary real well. You know how I thought the sun rose and set in her. What you don't know is that I almost let her get away from me the way you're letting Miss Becky get away from you now."

Jake leaned toward Sam. "It isn't the same thing at all, Sam. Mary loved you with all her heart."

"Yes, she did." The older man wiped an eye. "You know, Mr. Jake, that she was housekeeper and cook for your parents when I started working for your dad on the ranch. I tried to see her as often as I could, and she used to make me special food she never gave to the other hired hands. I took her dancing and to the picture shows. I loved her with all my heart. I wanted that sweet girl to be my wife, but I knew I wasn't good enough for her. One day, she up and takes another job clear over in Bozeman." Sam sat back in his chair. "I thought I'd die, but I had to let her go. I knew it was best for her. I could never offer her any more than she had working right here on this ranch."

"What made you change your mind?" Jake had never heard Sam's story before.

"One of the men here told me I had to go to Bozeman and bring her back. He said Mary loved me, and, if I'd only ask her, she'd be happy to marry me and live on this ranch." Sam inhaled deeply. "So I borrowed your dad's truck, and I went to Bozeman. I found Mary, and lost my nerve. I never even tried to talk to her. I turned around to go home, and a deputy sheriff stopped me. He took me to jail and called Mary to come get me out." Sam leaned forward. "You'd never guess why I was arrested."

"Speeding? Reckless driving?" Jake speculated.

"Nope," Sam said, folding his arms. "Your dad had a friend on the force in Bozeman, and he told the cops to look for me in his pickup. He told them if they found me alone instead of with Mary, they were to arrest me and call Mary to get me out. Then they weren't to let me go until I had asked Mary to be my wife."

Jake sprang to his feet. "You can't be serious! Dad did that? Why, that man never had a tender bone in his body."

"He did it, and I'm glad he did it. If it weren't for him, my stubbornness would have doomed me to a life without my Mary. It was because of your dad that I could live with Mary in that nice room I still have. She kept house, and I rode the range until she died, and I took over her job for you."

Jake put his hand on Sam's shoulder. "That's an amazing story, Sam. I'm glad you told me."

Sam stood. "Mr. Jake, you aren't going to let your Mary get away, are you?"

Jake shook his head. "Sam, Becky isn't Mary. She doesn't love me or the ranch. She has a life of her own. You've got to get that through your head."

"All right, Mr. Jake, if you won't go see her to bring her back, maybe you'll catch up to her to return those boots by the front door to her. She sets great store by them, and she happened to leave them. It would give you a chance to tell her good-bye too."

"Federal Express will give me the same opportunity. So will the US Postal Service. I'll send Becky's boots along with a farewell letter to her." Jake patted Sam's shoulder. "Sam, I know what you're trying to do, and I appreciate it." He walked toward the door and called over his shoulder. "I'll be in my office if you need anything."

Jake went straight to his office and opened up his word processor. He stretched and shook his head to clear his mind. He wrote: "Dear Mr. Jenkins." He paused, then walked to the window. He leaned against the sill and looked down the road leading away from his ranch. She was gone. He had to forget her.

Jake returned to his chair. He glanced around the room as he tried to think how to begin the letter. Suddenly, his eyes fell on a piece of paper that lay on the top of his trash can. He grabbed it and started to read:

Becca hadn't intended to fall in love, but she did. Jack had promised to marry someone else, though Becca loved him with all her heart. She wouldn't stop him. He'd made his choice. If he'd have loved her a little more, waited for her a moment longer, Becca would have never let him go. But life doesn't exist on if's, and Becca couldn't change fate. She'd lost Jack, and she'd never get him back. It was time to move on.

Jake folded the paper and shoved it into his pocket. He knew it had to be a segment of Becky's book, and it changed everything for him. Within seconds, he was at the bottom of the stairs. As he tore to the front door he shouted, "Sam, I'm going after Becky. You take care of things here." He picked up the boots next to the front door.

Sam instantly appeared at the kitchen door. "It's about time, Mr. Jake," he said, nearly laughing in his happiness. "I'd wish you good luck, but you don't need it. I already saw to that."

Jake had no idea what the old fellow was talking about, and he didn't have time to ask. Becky had a huge head start. He'd have to drive like a maniac and hope her flight was delayed.

He covered the territory leading to the airport faster than he'd ever managed to before. Halfway there, he saw something blocking the road ahead. He slammed his hand into the steering wheel. Why did someone have to be in trouble now of all times? He'd have to stop and help the person change his tire, or fix his engine, or whatever. He couldn't leave someone stranded.

As he neared the stalled car, he saw a woman leaning against the driver's door.

He got a little closer. It was Becky. The frustrated lines chiseled into his forehead disappeared as his lips curved into a smile. He pulled up behind Becky's car and parked his truck. He jumped out and walked toward her. "Having trouble, Becky?" he asked casually.

She folded her arms and held them tightly against herself. "I'm out of gas."

What a lucky break for him. "How long have you been waiting here?"

"Hours, I guess. I can't believe it. You're the first person to come by." Becky dropped her arms and shoved her thumbs into the back pockets of her jeans. "What brings you here?"

"Just a minute," he said, raising a finger. He sprinted back to the pickup and tugged out the pair of boots. Taking them back to Becky, he said, "You left these."

"My boots." She scowled up at Jake. "I know I had them with me. I even told Sam to double check when he loaded my luggage."

"You told Sam to check?" Jake asked, lifting a brow and grinning.

"Yes." She took the boots and tossed them into the car. "I guess next time I'll do the double checking myself." She looked back up at Jake. "Thanks for bringing them. I appreciate it."

"My pleasure," Jake said, smiling at her.

She wrinkled her nose and shielded her eyes against the sun. "I don't know how I could have run out of gas. I filled the tank yesterday. Do you suppose you could lend me enough to get to the airport?"

"Maybe," Jake said, folding his arms and looking at her very carefully. She filled the tank yesterday? Jake shifted his weight. Sam strikes again.

Becky dropped her body against the car. "Maybe? Oh, Jake, come on. I've been waiting here forever. You aren't out of gas too, are you?"

"No, I've got plenty." At least he didn't think Sam had siphoned off his tank as he apparently had done with Becky's.

Becky placed her hand over her heart. "Thank goodness." She straightened her stance. "Jake, I'm sorry about Catherine and Lucas."

He raked his hand through his hair. "Thanks, but I'm not." He lifted a shoulder. "I hope that things have worked out for the best."

"Me too." Becky tucked her hair behind her ears. "I hate to push you, Jake, but do you suppose I could get that gasoline now?" She glanced at her watch. "My flight leaves in an hour."

"In a minute," Jake said, studying her carefully. "First, I'd like to talk to you about this." He pulled the folded paper from his pocket and handed it to Becky.

She opened it and read her words. "This is the opening to my book." Becky wrinkled her forehead. "I thought I threw this in the trash can in my room."

"In your room? I found it on top of the trash can in my office." Then Jake remembered seeing that Sam had already cleaned the guest room when he went up to his office. He grinned and shook his head. "Strike three, Sam," he said inaudibly.

"Jake," Becky said, looking at him with confusion. "Is anything wrong?"

He straightened and rubbed a hand over his neck. "No, Becky, I think everything just might be right for the first time in weeks."

"Jake, you are exasperating!" Becky kicked the ground. "I don't have all day to stand here and go in circles."

"Maybe you don't," he said, taking her hands and letting the paper drift to the ground. He pulled her a bit closer to him. "Your story, the one about Jack and Becca, it's about us, isn't it? I mean Becca is like you and Jack is like me, right?"

"I don't know why you'd say that," she said demurely.

"Me either. It isn't as though the names are similar, is it?" He allowed ample sarcasm to mix with his words.

Becky grinned a soft touché.

He pulled her closer. "You do care about me, Becky, don't you?"

She cast her eyes downward, then back up at Jake. "Those boots in there," he said, nodding toward the car, "are anything but glass slippers, and I'm certainly no Prince Charming." He steadied her chin with one hand as he held her with the other. Her gaze fastened itself on him. He grinned down at her. "But we are like Becca and Jack. If I hadn't asked Catherine to marry me, you'd have given us a chance. Wouldn't you?"

Her eyes glistened as she blinked. "Maybe."

Jake lifted her hand to his lips and kissed her fingers lightly. "Becky, remember how I picked you up and carried you into my house the first time I saw you?"

She smiled a crooked smile and gave him an angular nod.

He kissed her fingers again. "Well, Becky, I want to take you in my arms and carry you over that threshold again. This time as my wife, going into *our* house."

Becky opened her mouth to speak, but Jake quickly dropped her hand and covered her lips with his fingers.

"Becky, I know you're afraid. You're scared that marriage for you might be a disaster like your parents' was. But I know that's impossible. Nothing bad could ever come of a love this good. And I do love you, Becky." He pulled her closer and encased her cheeks in his palms. "I love you with all my heart. It's the love of a man who knows exactly what he's doing, exactly what he wants, a man who comes to you completely open and unafraid and who hopes you want what he wants—for us to grow old together, in good times and bad, hand in hand, heart in heart, in love and friendship, until death parts us. Do you love me enough, Becky, to put your fear aside and trust me enough to give you a beautiful life?"

She looked at him carefully. "Oh, Jake," she said,

blinking back tears, "it sounds like a dream. If it is, don't wake me."

"It's no dream, Becky. It's real. I'll prove it." He lowered his lips to hers and savored the taste he'd longed for too many hours and days and nights. He pulled back and brushed his thumbs over her lips. "Do you believe me?"

She blinked back more tears. "I believe you, Jake, and I love you."

He bent his knees enough to bring himself to her eye level. "Then you'll marry me?"

She nodded inside the circle of his hands. "I'll marry you."

His face beamed as he stared at her for a long, quiet moment. "We can live in the city, if you want, New York or anywhere you'd like to live, Becky." He kissed her. "All I care about is being with you."

"Well," Becky said coyly as she pulled Jake's hands from her cheeks and took them into hers. "I suppose if you want to live in the city, I could stand it, but I'd really rather live on the ranch. It does wonders for a writer's inspiration."

Jake took a deep breath. "Well, I said I'd live anywhere with you, so if you want to live on the ranch, we'll live on the ranch."

Becky threw herself into Jake's arms and pressed him into her as tightly as she could. When she pulled back enough to look up into his eyes, she said, "Oh, Jake, I'm so happy, I don't know what to say."

He smiled down at her and brushed his palm over her cheek. "Then don't say anything, Becky," he whispered in his huskiest voice. He gazed at her with eyes full of love until her irresistible sweetness drew his lips to hers. Then he kissed her completely enough to seal their bargain permanently.

Shaff
Montana match

GAYLORD S